the breaking jewel

Makoto Oda

Translated by Donald Keene

columbia university press
new york

This publication has been supported by
the Rickard W. Weatherhead Publication Fund of
the East Asian Institute, Columbia University.

Columbia University Press
Publishers Since 1893
New York   Chichester, West Sussex

Library of Congress Cataloging-in-Publication Data
Oda, Makoto, 1932–
    [Gyokusai. English]
    The breaking jewel / Makoto Oda ; translated by
    Donald Keene.
      p.   cm. — (Weatherhead books on Asia)
    ISBN 0-231-12612-3 (cloth : alk. paper)
    ISBN 0-231-12613-1 (paper : alk. paper)
      I. Keene, Donald. II. Title. III. Series.

  PL858.D3 G96 2003
  895.6'35—dc21

                                      2002073430

∞

Columbia University Press books are printed
on permanent and durable acid-free paper.
Designed by Chang Jae Lee
Printed in the United States of America
c 10 9 8 7 6 5 4 3 2 1
p 10 9 8 7 6 5 4 3 2 1

the breaking jewel

weatherhead books on asia

WEATHERHEAD BOOKS ON ASIA
Columbia University

LITERATURE
David Der-wei Wang, Editor

Ye Zhaoyan, *Nanjing 1937: A Love Story*,
translated by Michael Berry

HISTORY, SOCIETY, AND CULTURE
Carol Gluck, Editor

Contents

Foreword

The earliest use of the word *gyokusai* is found in the biography of a Chinese of the sixth century (the northern Ch'i dynasty), who reportedly said that he would rather be a broken jewel than a whole tile, meaning that he would prefer to die gloriously than to live the inglorious life of a common clod. As adopted by the Japanese, the expression acquired a special meaning during the Pacific War. *Gyokusai* was used to describe the final, all-out charge of surviving Japanese units against superior American forces. The Americans called such actions "banzai charges" because many of the Japanese soldiers cried banzai as they made their suicidal charge into the teeth of enemy forces.

The impetus for such charges was the belief that it was nobler to offer one's life for one's country (and specifically for the emperor) than to cling shamefully to life. Of course, in every country the soldier who sacrifices his life for his country has been praised, but the *gyokusai* was not necessarily a last-ditch action; some were undertaken even when much longer resistance was possible. The readiness to die in an en masse attack was fostered by the creed inculcated in Japanese soldiers and sailors that in all their history, Japanese had never submitted to becoming prisoners of war. This was patently untrue. During the Russo-Japanese War, many Japanese soldiers (including officers) became prisoners and subsequently returned to Japan without suffering disgrace, but by the time of the Pacific War, the military authorities succeeded in convincing the Japanese of the existence of an unbroken tradition of choosing death rather than the humiliation of becoming prisoners.

I was present on the island of Attu in the northern Pacific at the time of the first *gyokusai* in April 1943. The Japanese garrison of some two thousand men was no match for the superior American forces that landed on the island. After putting up strong resistance, the Japanese decided to use all their remaining strength to stage a final attack. Perhaps they hoped that a sudden onslaught would sweep the Americans into the sea, but in fact American casualties remained light. Half the Japanese garrison died not from enemy action but from an act of mass suicide.

Most of the Japanese soldiers who were not killed in the final assault killed themselves, often by pressing a hand grenade to their chest. I was baffled by their determination to die, to use their last grenade against themselves rather than the enemy. Of course, the end of Japanese resistance on the island was welcome to the Americans, but the sight of the exploded corpses was sickening, and I found it impossible to reconcile what I interpreted as mindless fanaticism with what I knew of the Japanese from their works of literature.

The Japanese press (as I later discovered) acclaimed the *gyokusai* on Attu, declaring that not a single Japanese had survived. As a matter of fact, there were some prisoners—seven or eight men out of two thousand, including civilian employees of the Japanese navy. Colonel Yamazaki, the commander of the Japanese forces, was exalted as a model of heroic loyalty to the emperor. His fame reached even the countries of Southeast Asia occupied by the Japanese, and Indonesia's leading poet paid tribute not only to Yamazaki but also to the emperor. The *gyokusai* at Attu became a model for other Japanese garrisons to emulate, and there were repeated reports of "banzai charges."

Although Oda Makoto's novel is entitled *Gyokusai*, it describes not a *gyokusai* like the one on Attu but the prolonged resistance of Japanese soldiers who fought to the bitter end. The possibility of a *gyokusai* was, nonetheless, never far from their minds. Oda did extensive research before writing the work, but *Gyokusai* is a work of fiction, not a literal reconstruction of what happened on a particular island. In fact, Oda was at pains not to identify where the action took place, as if to reject any odor of wartime journalism. It was obvious to me, however, because of my experiences as a translator and interpreter during the war, that the place described in the novel is Peleliu, one of the Palau group, the island where the Japanese defenders put up the most prolonged and fiercest resistance to the American landing forces.

Oda's attention is focused especially on two men: Sergeant Nakamura, a soldier hardened by training in Manchuria who does not question the Japanese wartime ideals, and Corporal

Kon, a Korean serving in the Japanese army who aspires to be recognized as a worthy member of the emperor's forces.

In this and other of his works, Oda reveals a particular interest in the relations between Koreans and Japanese. Japan annexed Korea in 1910. Some Koreans, especially in the upper classes, were happy that an efficient Japanese regime had replaced the vacillating and corrupt rule of the Korean monarchy, but the vast majority of Koreans resented the dominance of the Japanese in their own country. In order to give legitimacy to its rule, the Japanese government insisted that the Japanese and the Koreans had the same ancestors and were, in essence, the same people. For this reason, the Japanese government ordered the Koreans to take Japanese surnames, to replace a typical Korean name like Kim with a Japanese name like Kanemura or Kaneyama. The use of the Korean language was frowned on and even forbidden, and everything else that distinguished Koreans from Japanese was downplayed.

If these measures had actually been intended to promote feelings of solidarity between Koreans and Japanese, they might eventually have been successful, but from the first it was clear that the Koreans under Japanese rule were to be no more than a colonized people. The name Korea was avoided, and Koreans were known merely as "peninsula people," denying that they had a nationality of their own. All the same, far from treating the Koreans as equals, the Japanese made fun of their awkward pronunciation of Japanese, complained of their garlicky breath, and otherwise looked down on the Koreans as lazy, stupid, and unclean. These prejudices have not yet disappeared but were at their height in the 1920s when the militarists achieved dominance in Japan. The dislike of Koreans came to a head after the Great Earthquake of 1923 when Koreans were lynched in Tokyo on suspicion of having poisoned the wells. Even today, when such overt discrimination is much diminished, many Japanese are shocked when they learn that a neighbor or a classmate or an acquaintance, long supposed to be a fellow Japanese, is actually Korean.

Corporal Kon (he insists on pronouncing his name in the Japanese manner rather than as Kim) is determined to beat the Japanese at their own game by proving he is the best soldier in the regiment. It was unusual for Koreans to be inducted on active duty with the Japanese forces. Instead, most were civilian employees required to perform labor for the military. Many of the "Japanese" prisoners during the first years of the war were in fact Korean laborers, mustered in their villages and sent to the islands of the Pacific to build airfields or harbor facilities. Kon, however, insists that he is a Japanese soldier, even though he comes from "the peninsula." He is proud that other Koreans are now serving like himself in the Japanese forces. He is fighting not only the Americans but the prejudices of the Japanese, resolved to win recognition as their equal.

Private Second Class Kaneshiro, whom Kon takes under his wing, is an Okinawan. Japanese from the main islands grudgingly admitted that Okinawans were Japanese, but at the time of the novel (and even much later) they were subjected to almost as much discrimination as the Koreans. Their prefecture was the poorest, and the Okinawans were looked down on for such reasons as that they preferred pork to fish, unlike "real" Japanese. *Gyokusai* is given complexity by the irony that Koreans and Okinawans were offering their lives to save a country that did not recognize them as its own.

Oda Makoto, the author, was born in Osaka in 1932. As a boy of thirteen, he witnessed the destruction of his native city by American bombers, an experience that recurs in his writings. After the war, he wandered through the black markets that sprang up in Osaka and saw the degeneration of the wartime ideals. Later, in his novels, he vividly recalled these scenes. Oda dropped out of school and seemed to have lost all interest in the traditional Japanese struggle to get ahead in society. He was rescued from this apathy by the discovery of the new literature that first appeared in the postwar era. Oda thereupon returned to school, and by the time he reached high school, he was not only writing poetry and prose but sending it to senior writers for their comments.

In 1952 Oda entered Tokyo University to study classical Greek. He published his first novel in 1956 while still a student. In the following year he graduated from the university with a thesis on Longinus. Two years later, he received a Fulbright fellowship to continue his study of Greek at Harvard. He took advantage of his stay in America to see as much of the country as possible, showing boundless curiosity about everything he saw. After returning to Japan in 1960, he published *I'll Look at Anything,* a book that describes his travels in the United States, Canada, and Mexico. It became a popular success and launched Oda on a career as a writer.

His next work, the novel *America,* begun while at Harvard, dealt with the problem of racial prejudice. He seemed to have abandoned his study of ancient Greece, but in 1963 he published *The Death of Socrates,* evidence that his increasing preoccupation with political and social problems had not blotted out his old interests. A series of volumes of essays followed in which he voiced his concerns with nationalism, the problems of Asia and Africa, and the postwar experience as a whole. His political views became increasingly radical but not dogmatic; his writings remained idiosyncratic rather than doctrinaire even when he wrote about his principal concern, the war in Vietnam. In 1965 he and several like-minded friends founded the Peace for Vietnam Committee (Beheiren), of which he was known as the guiding spirit. In this capacity he organized mass meetings at which peace in Vietnam was demanded, and he was known for his efforts to help American deserters find refuge in neutral countries. He continued to involve himself in these and related activities until the left-wing ideologues began to go their separate ways. Taking a wholly independent line, Oda shifted the emphasis in his work from organizing protest meetings to writing criticism.

Oda's outspoken attacks on American foreign policy, and particularly on the role of the United States in Vietnam, were perhaps not surprising in view of his childhood experiences of war. He was at the same time strongly attracted to America, especially to its cultural freedom, and spent years in America as a visiting professor. His interest in ancient Greece revived once again when he published a new translation of Longinus's *On the Sublime,* the theme of his graduation essay.

Today Oda is a prominent, if controversial, figure in the Japanese literary world. His writings have won major literary prizes in Japan, and some have been translated into European languages and into Korean. This is his first novel to be translated into English.

Donald Keene

the breaking jewel

"Sergeant Nakamura," Kon suddenly called out. Nakamura had just ordered the members of his squad to leave the cave where they had been constructing a fortified position and take a break on the outside. Kon, a noncommissioned officer attached to the squad, looked up at Sergeant Nakamura, who had seated himself on a mud-smeared rock to the side. Kon had settled on the ground by the entrance to the cave. The ground was damp and shining with mud.

Kon's voice was low, but it carried well. Here and there in this patch of grassy land, a fairly big gap in the jungle, soldiers were relaxing in whatever way they felt most comfortable, some sitting, some stretched out, all greedily savoring the brief respite. Something in their attitudes indicated to Kon that they were straining to hear what he would say next. He noticed that several men, heads lifted, were shifting their glances back and forth between Kon to Nakamura as if comparing the two men. A weird-looking bird that nested in the jungle passed overhead, emitting eerie squawks, each time more sharply penetrating, a strange cry like the howling of an infant. There was a rustling sound as the bird's wings struck the unyielding foliage of a tree in the jungle. The sound echoed loudly in the bottomless depths of luxuriant growth.

"Sergeant, about that meeting early this morning," Kon began, turning his head and looking back at the cave, "you passed on to us the commander's instructions-dig, hide, stay alive, fight. Those were his four points, right?"

Kon and Nakamura both had begun to smoke. The smell and smoke of Golden Bat cigarettes drifted between them. Kon looked at Nakamura intently from his side of the smoke.

"You've got the general idea, Corporal Kon. But you left out one item."

Nakamura gazed across the drifting smoke at Kon's face, sunburned a coppery red, and his unusually big head: a head so big that according to Kon, it was twice normal size, and for this reason he had never found a military cap, field cap, or helmet to fit it. Both Kon and Nakamura were aware that the others were listening. The puzzled expression on Kon's face showed he was trying to figure out what he had omitted. Nakamura, responding to this look of uncertainty, spoke quietly, brushing away the swarm of flies that clustered on his face the instant he took the cigarette from his mouth. One reason why Nakamura and all the other soldiers smoked incessantly in the jungle was to keep the flies from covering their faces.

"It was, we must win . . . Digging holes, building positions, hiding in them, staying alive and fighting-all will lead to final victory. The commanding officer called us squad leaders together, and those were his instructions. I thought I'd passed on to you, Corporal Kon, the commanding officer's words, exactly as he said them, this morning while we were constructing the retrenchment. . . ."

Nakamura punctiliously pronounced the word "retrenchment," the technical military term for a fortified cave, and then, continuing, drove home the point for Kon's benefit: "I suppose you know, but we in the garrison of this island have not been sent to the South Pacific to dig holes simply so we can die in them. The positions we build are not graves, and we're not grave diggers. The motto of us members of the island garrison is that we will build with our bodies a bulwark of the Pacific Ocean, and by building a bulwark of the Pacific Ocean we can serve the Imperial Throne. But that holds only if we fight and win. The garrison is digging holes and constructing positions so we can win the war."

His voice had imperceptibly filled with anger. Nakamura poured out his words in one unbroken flow, without knowing what was annoying him. His voice became excited. He had even come to feel as if he were spurring himself on.

Kon said nothing, but Nakamura could tell from the expression on his face that he did not consider that Nakamura had got the best of him in this discussion. There were signs of annoyance in Kon's expression as well. Probably he had also become angry without knowing why.

After a few minutes of silence, Kon said abruptly, to nobody in particular, "I'm going to win. I fully intend to." He also seemed to be directing his words to himself. He said "I'm going to win," stressing the I, not "We're going to win." Nakamura heard Kon's words distinctly and caught the implications.

"And that's exactly why I'm digging holes. I'm giving everything I've got to digging. The holes I dig are not going to be my grave. I'll be fighting from them. They'll be the positions where I make my stand."

Kon emphasized each word. He seemed to be chopping out the words, one after the other, pushing them from his mouth. Each time he uttered the word "I," he gave it particular emphasis.

The bird flew overhead again howling like a baby or, rather, like the shrieking of a strangled baby in its last agony. It flew off. This time it seems to have been more successful in flying through the complicated intertwinings of jungle growth—there was no sound of wings crashing against the foliage. The jungle was absolutely still.

"End of break." Nakamura called in a loud voice, brushing away with his fist the flies that persistently swarmed over his face.

"Resume construction of retrenchment positions. All hands, back to work."

Nakamura stood up. It was getting close to the time in the afternoon when day after day, the enemy air attacks began. First the B-17 bombers would fly over, dropping bombs, and then Grumman fighters would strafe with their machine guns. This was just the time of day for the attacks. Their best plan was to get back into the cave—or, rather, the retrenchment—and resume work.

"Dig those holes! And put everything you've got into it!"

With these words, delivered in tones as cheerful as he could manage, Nakamura started walking toward the mouth of the cave. It was covered by a thick curtain of innumerable hanging, intertwined strands of ferns. With the deftness and agility of bodily movement that marked him as a veteran soldier, Kon lightly picked himself up from the muddy ground, and with a practiced gesture that suggested he might be brushing aside the rope curtain at the entrance of a favorite drinking place somewhere, he pushed through the hanging ferns. The next instant he had half disappeared inside the cave.

 2

Constructing a position certainly did involve digging holes; it might be called a hole-digging operation.

The mobilization order sending them to an island in the South Pacific for garrison duty had been issued back in March when in the bitter cold of northern Manchuria, masses of snow still lingered unmelted in the open spaces between the barracks buildings. They had left the division post and proceeded toward their new assignment on transports that passed Japan without landing anywhere. (The ships entered port at three places in Japan, but going ashore was not permitted. The last place the ship called was near the region where many soldiers of the island garrison, including Nakamura, came from, but the best they could do was stand on the deck and stare at the green mountains, as if trying to engrave the outlines in their memories.) Once the ships moved out to the open sea, enemy planes and submarines were in control, and the convoy had to take evasive action and backtrack at the approach of an enemy task force. It took a whole month before the ships at last reached the main island of the Palau group, where the area's headquarters were located. From there they were carried on landing barges another forty-odd kilometers south to Peleliu, a small island eight kilometers long and three kilometers at its widest point. That was four months ago, and ever since then the garrison had been practicing counterattacks against projected enemy landings. At breaks in between the daily bombing raids by B-17 bombers and Grumman fighters, they had devoted all their energy to hacking and breaking the reef along the shore to make air-raid shelters, trenches, and tank traps. They put up obstacles of every kind in the water and on the shore. They stretched numerous strands of barbed wire. They constructed pillboxes at different places, then dug tunnels to connect them. As they worked, they could see out of the corners of their eyes the beach, the sand shining silvery white in the tropical sunlight, and, on the far side of the glittering sand, the coral reef and the intense, unearthly blue of the sea. The purpose of these fortifications was to annihilate the enemy landing force at the water's edge.

When excavation work on the shoreline had been completed for the time being, the construction of positions shifted to the jungle in the center of the island and to the central mountainous area. The men went into the caves, which spread in all directions under the jungle as far as the base of the steep ridges of the central mountainous area. Inhabited by innumerable bats, poisonous snakes, scorpions, poisonous lizards, and little poisonous insects called chiggers, the caves were dark even during the day, or, it might more accurate to say, the caves for the most part were darkness itself. The men excavated and widened the caves and, making do with insufficient materials, installed wooden columns, wooden boards, reinforcing rods, steel frames, and sheet iron. They poured in concrete, strengthening the rock bed and the rock walls. This was the first stage of all the retrenchment constructions.

The basic preparations, whether for field positions on the shoreline reefs or retrenchments in the caves of the central area, were carried out by engineers with professional competence. Up until just a year or two earlier, the island had been actively used as a major facility by the area's naval base flying corps. Three or four hundred construction workers had been mobilized from the home islands, Okinawa, and Korea to build the airfield where now a few Zero fighters, all of them old and battered, were kept hidden with fanatical care in the jungle near the landing strip. Because no plane or ship had ever come to take the construction workers back home, they were still on the island; but with barely a couple of hundred workers as a labor force, it was most unlikely that the island, virtually defenseless when Nakamura and the others arrived in April, could quickly be turned into a fortress. Of necessity, the entire garrison force that arrived in April was put to work building fortifications. They had almost no construction machinery. All they had were pickaxes, hammers, shovels, a small amount of dynamite (but they were under orders to use manpower insofar as possible and to save the dynamite), straw baskets for carrying excavated earth and rocks, wooden boards, and buckets. What was worse, this work, done entirely by hand, had to be carried out during intervals between counterattack drills (20 percent drilling and 80 percent fatigue duty), and evasive action had to be repeated every time one of the daily American air attacks occurred.

They had been told at first that provisions were assured for the entire garrison for nine months and that supplies of water were sufficient, but shipments from the main island had gradually fallen behind schedule, no doubt because enemy planes and submarines controlled the skies and seas. "Save Food! Save Water!" was now the watchword, and it was plain to the men, especially in their stomachs, how much worse conditions had become. Again and again, complaints were heard even from soldiers of the garrison, though they had been hardened in the bitter cold of Manchuria and by the regiment's tradition of outstanding bravery dating back to the Russo-Japanese War. This had become a topic of discussion among the squad leaders of Nakamura's company, but it was no longer merely a topic of conversation. It was a problem.

Nakamura's squad also included men who complained, "I didn't join the army to be a construction worker in a place like this." There were even some like Saeki who came out with such stupidities as "If this is the best we can expect, I wish Mr. Enemy would hurry up and come. I'd be happy to get killed by a bullet from Mr. Enemy, the sooner the better." Saeki was a reserve conscript with a wife and child. Before getting conscripted, he had run a laundry. Nakamura paid no attention to the complaints of the former variety, but he couldn't very well keep silent in Saeki's case. He gave the reservist (who was three years older than himself) a stiff talking-to, then slapped his face. This had an effect on the morale of the whole squad. Nakamura, really angry, demanded, "What do you mean talking like a spoiled brat?" As a squad leader he was reputed never to lay a finger on a subordinate except in the most extraordinary circumstances. Behind his back, his men called their squad leader by the nickname Momotarō-san, meaning he was strong but gentle. This time, the man he had slapped desperately apologized, imploring to be forgiven,

"Mr. Squad Leader, First Class Private Saeki made a mistake. I apologize."

Saeki had once shown him a close-up photograph of his wife holding in her arms a cute little boy about five years old. "This is my son," he said. The wife looked as if she had a firm character, but Saeki said with a touch of pride that deep down she was really sweet. It lasted only a moment, but Nakamura felt as if something had got into him. He wished he had a family like that. Then he mercilessly began to administer furious, open-hand slaps to Saeki's face, feeling all the greater pity for the reservist who had left behind such a family, far off in Japan.

Each slap delivered with full force by Nakamura caused the body of short-statured Private First Class Saeki to shake helplessly. "Don't stagger that way. Keep standing straight and dig in your heels. Take my slaps like a man," Nakamura roared at him, putting even more force into his slaps. "Do you suppose that by talking that way we can beat the American devils? Do you think you can die for His Majesty the Emperor and become a bulwark of the Pacific?" Nakamura, acting as if he had gone out of his senses, went on slapping and screaming at the same time.

From the time he was in northern Manchuria and the command came down sending them to the South Pacific, Nakamura himself had heard on the transport and since reaching the island—often enough to get calluses on his ears—the transport commander, the battalion commander, the company commander, the platoon commander, and every other superior officer say that the motto of the island garrison was "My body will be a bulwark of the Pacific." He had repeated it to his men, but to tell the truth, he didn't like this watchword. As a matter of fact, he disliked it. It was passive, somehow. That was something about it that seemed to say that a man must stand firm, even though he could foresee that his side, being in a position of inferiority, would lose the war. The words certainly conveyed adequately the grit needed to hold firm, to dig in, but it said nothing about the grit needed to take the initiative and vigorously launch an attack on the enemy. At any rate, not enough. Even if in obedience to the motto, they dug holes with everything they had, it was not made clear enough that the purpose of this hole digging was to enable their side to come out of the holes and fight. Somewhere or other in the words, the feeling was communicated of digging one's own grave. It hovered around the words "My body will be a bulwark of the Pacific." This is how Nakamura took the words. Now the stormy waves, the huge waves of the enemy's material superiority, breaking against bulwarks all over the Pacific, were about to crash over them. Nakamura wanted something more positive. He yearned for it desperately with his whole body—a body encased in a uniform that was old, torn in places, and stained by sweat and by sand and mud from the positions they had been constructing.

 3

The address of instructions delivered just a couple of days ago by the force commander to the assembled squad leaders of the entire garrison had given Nakamura strength and hope. The talk, which lasted a little less than an hour, was delivered inside a cave at the base of a particularly steep cliff, a sheer drop of some thirty meters, that stood out even among the precipices of the central mountainous region. During breaks between air attacks, the men had completed a multiple position here, to serve as an underground command post in the event that the fighting developed into a war of attrition. After the commander's talk, Nakamura felt as if he had received, for the first time in a long while, the spirit of victory, the confidence that they would win the war. This is why he could feel cheerful as he pushed his way out of the cave at the base of the precipice, through the vines and creepers hanging over the mouth.

It had been a long time since they last were given instructions by a high-ranking officer, whether the force commander or anybody else, not since the day before they moved out, bound for the South Pacific, in accordance with mobilization orders. There was still snow on the ground in Manchuria, and a cold wind was raging. They had been made to stand for hours in the barracks square of the post to hear the division commander deliver an inspirational talk to all the men bound for the front. Of course, it hadn't been possible to give such talks on the cramped deck of a transport, and ever since coming to the island, they been so frantically busy with drills and work parties that there had been neither the time nor the place for anything as leisurely as a pep talk to the assembled troops by the force commander. Hardly—if anything of the kind had been tried, Grumman fighters would soon have mowed them all down in one blast of machine-gun strafing, and the lot of them would have achieved, without doing another thing, a *gyokusai*, "the breaking of the jewel."

Nakamura remembered perfectly the speech the division commander had delivered when the troops were about to leave their post in northern Manchuria for the front. The speech had later been mimeographed and distributed to squad leaders with instructions that they were to make sure that all members of their squads were thoroughly familiar with the contents. It opened with the usual stereotyped expressions: "You who have come forward loyally and with true sincerity to serve in this hour of our country's need, pledging one another you will 'smite and destroy the enemy' and will 'not return if not victorious,' have now completed various, extremely difficult preparations before you depart for the front." The commander then proceeded to enumerate in truly hackneyed terms what was expected of them: "The true significance of our holy war has permeated the hearts of staff officers and below, and each of you, down to the humblest soldier, as a member of the army of Jimmu,* must display faithfully the will of the gods. A soldier always recognizes the place where he is to die. To go into the jaws of death cheerfully, at a word of command, is to live for a great and eternal cause. Each and every one of you, prepared for death as you advance, must take it on yourself to break through whatever obstacles lie in your path and sacrifice yourself joyfully for your country in this time of crisis."

The mimeographed text was not punctuated but ran on without a break between words or sentences. Such admonitions might have affected Nakamura when as a young soldier on active duty who had joined the army with hope and expectations, he had found everything new and exciting, but

*The legendary first emperor of Japan.

in the years that followed he had heard stereotyped pronouncements of this variety from superior officers so often that he was sick of them; they obviously could not stir the heart of a veteran like himself. Many of the mimeographed sheets of paper distributed to each squad leader had ended up being stuffed into the trash incinerator in a corner of the barracks yard.

However, the speech of instructions delivered in the cave by the garrison commander was totally unlike such strings of platitudes. It was decisively different in both language and content—no, in the very fact that it had content.

The command for all squad leaders to assemble had suddenly been received the day before. The next morning, when Nakamura entered the cave that was intended to serve as an underground command post, he was surprised, first of all, that the construction of the cave as a retrenchment had been completed. He had never previously entered the cave, although he had passed it a couple of times. The cave, people said, was the biggest in the area. Nakamura was surprised to see not only that the interior, for the most part, had been reinforced with concrete but also that the rock wall had been knocked down here and there to form rooms. The air inside was heavy with the sour smell of concrete mingling with the smell of creosote disinfectant, no doubt because field hospital facilities had already been installed somewhere. A noncommissioned officer, an acquaintance of Nakamura's whom he ran into accidentally on entering the huge installation, informed him that it contained not only a provisions depot but water storage tanks. This senior corporal, attached to headquarters, whispered into Nakamura's ear with a self-satisfied look on his face that if they were holed up here, they could last a whole year. "What do you mean, 'last'?" Nakamura retorted with annoyance.

The lecture took place in one corner of the cave. It was in itself big enough to be taken for headquarters. The squad leaders, who had been ordered late the previous night to assemble on the double the next morning, were lined up now in three rows in order of seniority, waiting under the dim light of an electric bulb lit by an independent power generator. Presently the sound of military boots could be heard from the darkness at the back of the cave, and the commanding officer appeared, accompanied by a young adjutant. The general had gained a reputation for fearless leadership as the commanding officer of a punitive force during the bandit-suppression campaign in China, and that was undoubtedly why he had been chosen to head this division, with its tradition of outstanding bravery. The garrison would defend this small island to the death, faithful to the spirit of "My body will be a bulwark of the Pacific Ocean."

After taking the salutes of the rows of squad leaders, the general briefly thanked them for their trouble in coming. His talk began with introductory remarks explaining why he had asked them to assemble. The present operation was of vital importance. This was why, though it was not customary, he wanted them, the frontline leaders, to be informed of the essentials of the operational plan. Before launching into the talk proper, he said one more thing to the rows of squad leaders: "Come closer!" He directed his adjutant to get the frontline leaders to form a circle around him. This also was a departure from normal practice.

This disregard of precedent by the commanding officer won the heart of frontline leader Nakamura. He stared intently at the officer's face, barely visible in the dim light of a naked electric bulb. His lower jaw was noticeably unshaven, and fatigue marked his overall expression, but even though he lacked vitality, his face, with its prominent cheekbones and sharply glittering eyes under heavy eyebrows, suggested a powerful will. At the post in northern Manchuria, Nakamura had hardly ever seen the commanding officer except for the time he gave the final instructions to the troops. As he watched this officer's face at close range, the thought suddenly flitted across Nakamura's mind that this was the face of a "warrior," to use the old expression.

The "warrior" clenched with his right hand the hilt of a saber that he had firmly planted against the rock bed of the cave. From time to time he used his left fist to wipe the sweat trickling down his cheeks, speaking all the while slowly and forcefully in a deep, husky voice. His looks and manner of speaking were exactly right for a "warrior." The recognition came from the depths of Nakamura's heart.

"Our empire, Japan, is in the midst of a desperate struggle. You all know this without my having to tell you."

The "warrior" spoke brusquely to the circle of frontline squad leaders assembled around him. The straightforward manner with which he began his speech also was a departure from the usual rhetoric. Nakamura tensely waited for the next words. The "warrior" continued in the same deep, husky voice, "You have come to this island prepared for a fight to the death. That . . ." For a moment the "warrior" broke off, only to resume immediately, "is true of me too."

Having heard this much, Nakamura instantly guessed that he would next hear the stock phrases the men had always heard from superior officers, like those in the speech the commanding general of the division gave when they were about to leave northern Manchuria—"I have taken your lives into my hands. Follow me!" But the words the "warrior" actually said in the same powerful tones were not those Nakamura had expected: "A fight to the death does not mean being in a hurry to commit *gyokusai,* a *gyokusai* like dying a dog's death."

These words came as a surprise not only to Nakamura but to the squad leaders around him, as he could tell from the slight stirring among them. These old-timers, frontline leaders who had seen combat of every conceivable description over the years, were not to be moved by the usual platitudes. But now they clearly had begun to listen attentively.

The "warrior" who was their commanding officer resumed, saying that a *gyokusai* took resolution, but a *gyokusai* whose only justification was that it was a *gyokusai* was meaningless. He related the story of a certain island where the fighting had ended with a general *gyokusai.* The commander of a battalion that had suffered heavy casualties immediately after the American landing managed to extract reluctant permission from headquarters for a *gyokusai* attack. After barely a day of fighting, the battalion staged a *gyokusai* night attack and was wiped out. This inevitably speeded up the *gyokusai* of the whole island.

"I don't know what others may say, but as far as I am concerned, that kind of *gyokusai* is a dog's death of a *gyokusai.*"

He emphasized the words "dog's death." While pronouncing these words with emphasis, he stared straight ahead. In front of him was the circle of squad leaders, Nakamura and the rest, but Nakamura suddenly felt that the commander's eyes were no longer on them. Then what was he looking at?

"What is the purpose of *gyokusai* attacks? Isn't it so we can win? Isn't that why we head, ready to be annihilated, into the final battle? It's not to get killed. *Gyokusai* attacks are carried out in order to bring about victory. Otherwise, no matter how many times we may repeat *gyokusai* attacks, they won't drive off the enemy. And we won't succeed in making our bodies bulwarks of the Pacific."

The commanding officer's words powerfully shook Nakamura by the clearly defined link he established between *gyokusai* and victory. *Gyokusai,* as he explained in his speech, was not passive. It was not a last-ditch act of desperation, proof (if nothing else) of having held out to the end though in the hopeless situation of being cornered by the enemy and having nowhere to escape. It must be a more positive, dynamic act aimed at pushing back the enemy by charging out and beating him to the punch. The commanding officer's words made Nakamura feel as if he could clearly see himself fighting as a positive and dynamic act, the final battle of a *gyokusai.* The situation was desperate, of course. But even in that situation he would fight with a distinct objective before him. He could see himself fighting. The objective would be, of course, victory. He felt as if the doubts that had lurked in the depths of his heart had for the first time cleared. With bolstered spirits he stared at the commanding officer, who, looking exactly like a "warrior," in turn continued to stare before him. Now Nakamura himself had become a "warrior." He saw himself in the role.

4

Continuing his candid presentation of the situation, the "warrior" declared that the interception tactics
that had been employed on various islands against enemy
landings had failed in every case. This was because the Japanese forces were so intent on destroying the enemy at the
water's edge that they mistakenly adopted the plan of charging at the enemy, paying no attention to the endless waves of
enemy land-based bombers, the bombing and strafing by carrier planes, and the overwhelmingly strong firepower sup-
porting the enemy landing force, the tons or even dozens of
tons of explosives that each second were indiscriminately
thrown into the attack. In face of this enormous firepower,
the garrison, having already exposed itself plainly as being
without cover or protective walls, had suffered numerous casualties in a few hours and had completely lost its fighting capacity when it faced the invaders; the result of the contest
was thus foreordained. The defenders would decide on a
gyokusai after a day or two, at best after a few days, a week,
two weeks, three weeks. "The battalion I mentioned a moment ago was an extreme case, but it is now a major question
for our army why the garrison of a big island, the northern
strong point of this whole area, where the largest possible
military strength—though still far from sufficient—had been
concentrated, a place said to be impregnable, where they had
boldly adopted a plan of destroying the enemy at the water's
edge and not allowing one American soldier ashore, in less
than a month was driven to *gyokusai*." The force commander did not mention the name of the big island, but of course
it was a name that everybody already knew. On this big is-

land there were many resident Japanese, and it wasn't only the garrison that committed *gyokusai*. The Japanese residents, including women and children, all threw themselves from cliffs, giving their lives for the everlasting great cause. Nakamura had heard about this.

The force commander's unsparing analysis of the situation was delivered in severe tones. If there was something to be said, he said it without circumlocutions, no matter what the subject might be. The man's mettle permeated his tone. "I have no intention of disparaging the officers and men of that island. They fought well. They fought and they died." He repeatedly injected phrases of this kind into his talk, but his concern for the reputations of those who had died was unnecessary. He mentioned these events as his particular problem, the fate that every member of the garrison of this small island, including himself, would soon come up against, perhaps with the same result. His earnestness permeated both his expression and his voice. Nakamura and each of the other squad leaders heard his words as their personal problem.

"Then, what are we to do?" the commanding officer said, as if asking himself. The wrinkle between his eyebrows was plainly visible even in the dim light.

He replied slowly to his own question, as if testing his answer. "We have only one course of action." Then he added, "As far as I am aware." Nakamura thought there was something funny in this qualification, and it made him feel affection for the man.

"First of all," the officer continued, "we should conceal ourselves in the strong field positions that the garrison with its every ounce of strength has constructed along the shore and wait there patiently and cautiously for the enemy to land.

The bombing from the air and the naval bombardment will be extremely intense before the American forces land, but as long as we are protected by solidly built fortifications, we will not suffer major damage. We know this from the lessons that have been learned from battles fought on other islands. In short, the big question is whether or not we have the spiritual strength to endure this test psychologically. Hundreds of landing craft and amphibious vehicles, together with amphibious tanks, will blast their way through the coral reef, or they may go over it and swarm over our beaches. But we mustn't be in too big a hurry. If we start firing too soon, the next thing we know we'll be getting air strikes and naval bombardment. When the landing craft and amphibious vehicles reach the beach line and the American troops have started to go ashore, the first wave of the attacking army will have reached a point where they are too close for the Americans to carry out air strikes or naval bombardment. When their position is from one hundred to one hundred fifty meters from the shoreline, the front line of our coast defenses will simultaneously begin firing—field guns, infantry guns, quick-firing guns, antitank guns, horizontal firing antiaircraft guns, pom-poms, trench mortars, and every other kind of weapon we have kept concealed and ready in our field positions. At the same time, we should come out for hand-to-hand fighting with machine guns, rifles, and grenade throwers. This strategy of annihilating the enemy at the water's edge will in itself be a great success, and we should be able to repel the first one or two waves of the landing. We certainly can do that. All the same, the Americans have material superiority. Even after we've won a big victory, annihilating them at the water's edge, they may succeed in securing a landing point somewhere else on the coast. But on the first day of the landing, the enemy shore defenses still won't be too strong. Our battle experiences on other islands has made this clear. The key to victory will be a night attack in the traditions of our Imperial Army, carried out from night until dawn the next morning with the full strength of our coastal garrison against the enemy's shore defenses. It will be mainly an infiltration attack, and in addition to the weapons normally carried on in night attacks—machine guns, rifles, and grenade throwers—every kind of weapon our garrison has available—including engineering explosive throwers, naval bomb launchers, flamethrowers—will be mobilized. This night attack will be launched against their shore defenses with everything we've got. Once we've broken through the enemy's perimeter, we should immediately charge from the rear. By dawn the next morning, we'll have destroyed the enemy forces in the shore emplacements and made a clean sweep of them."

Having delivered in one breath the details of how the enemy would be annihilated at the water's edge, the commanding officer concluded in the tones of a "warrior": "In warfare there's something called a victory chance. If you miss the chance, you can't win, no matter how big the army you may pour into the fight. Even a few soldiers, if they seize the chance, can get the better of the enemy and win a victory."

"Our enemies, the Americans, will attack, brandishing long spears. The weapons our army will fight them with will be short swords. We'll wait, not getting upset by the power of their long spears, until the enemy comes within range of our short swords. We'll wait patiently, and when the time comes, we'll boldly take our short swords in hand and, in one powerful thrust, drive them into the throats of our spear-carrying enemies. In a battle at the water's edge, there are only two possibilities—either a sweeping victory or total defeat. Which will it be, a complete, heroic victory or total defeat? Everything will be decided between the time the Americans land and dawn the next morning. Will we or won't we be able make ourselves into bulwarks of the Pacific? Can we repay the immeasurable debt we owe His Majesty and set his heart at ease? Everything depends on that one night and the desperate determination of every man in the coastal garrison, ready to step over the corpses of his comrades to do battle. If this chance for victory is missed, no matter how famous we may become later for our courage in carrying out a *gyokusai,* it will have no meaning. No meaning at all."

The calm tone with which the commanding officer had begun his remarks displayed the self-possession of the "warrior," but as he went on, his words became vehement, transmitting to them the full strength of his uprush of emotion. Until this point he had delivered an unbroken monologue, all the while looking around the circle of squad leaders, but now he broke off his words and again stared straight before him. The stare bespoke a kind of hesitation. Nakamura happened to notice it. But immediately afterward, the commanding officer, as if pushing from him the hesitation, resumed his talk, again looking around the circle of men. Nakamura momentarily caught the movements of the ever-watchful commanding officer's eyes as he quickly sized up the reactions of the circle around him.

"However," he declared, "victory or defeat ultimately depends on the fortunes of the moment. No matter how much we exert our every effort, it may happen that if the will of the gods is not with us, we won't win the battle."

The commanding officer returned his gaze to the eyes of the men staring straight at him.

"In that case, what are we to do?" The commanding officer spoke slowly, as if once again asking himself the question. He also seemed to be asking the circle of squad leaders.

The circle maintained its silence.

"Our entire garrison will, without any hesitation, withdraw to rear areas and shift its strategy to a war of attrition in depth."

The commanding officer spoke in such a way that his words could be taken either as a command to the circle of silent squad leaders or merely as information for their benefit. It was in order to be able to carry out an in-depth operation of attrition that the garrison, after erecting field positions on the coastline, had thrown its full strength into constructing retrenchment positions to serve as the bases for such an operation, making use of the system of caves that stretched from under the jungle area as far as the rocky cliffs of the central mountainous region. The garrison had already constructed up to five hundred retrenchment positions, ranging from big caves that would serve as underground command posts in the event of a war of attrition down to caves that were so small they could hold only a couple of soldiers, but the number of positions was still far from sufficient. "Greater efforts than ever are demanded of you . . ." the commanding officer continued, once again speaking in a manner that might be interpreted as either a command or merely information. "During the day you will hide in the retrenchment positions, but at night you will emerge from the caves to stage attacks of infiltration, and these night attacks, in the traditions of the Imperial Army, will wear down the enemy. Then, when the time comes, but only then, with ultimate victory as its goal, the entire garrison will stage a *gyokusai* attack and fall like flowers over the Pacific Ocean." With these words, he concluded his talk.

After he had finished speaking, the commanding officer's expression, which up to this point had been severe, softened slightly as if he felt satisfied he had said everything that needed saying. There were quite a few white hairs mixed among the black in the scraggly growth of beard on his lower jaw. Nakamura wondered how old this "warrior" might be.

After a brief silence, the commanding officer resumed, emphasizing his words: "As I mentioned at the outset of these instructions, a commanding officer would never, except under the most exceptional circumstances, ask frontline leaders like yourselves to come before him and brief them directly on the plan of operations. A subordinate, no matter who he may be, must fight, at the risk of his life, once the force commander, the highest officer in command, issues an order, and for this reason, as force commander, I have never done anything like this before. However, I have chosen to take this step because the battle, both offensive and defensive, for this small island will be of decisive importance in breaking the present, painful deadlock in the Greater East Asia War."

The softness visible a moment before in the commander's expression had disappeared. He continued, "The essential thing at this point is for all members of the garrison—regardless of whether they are officers, noncommissioned officers, or enlisted men—to be united as one and for each and every man to fight not merely with confidence in victory— that goes without saying—but with the strategy and tactics he has made a part of himself in order to ensure victory. Each and every man, even if he's the last surviving soldier, will fight on. He will fight and win. Only if he is imbued with both the spirit and the techniques to fight on, even if he's alone, can ultimate victory be won in the fight for this small island. In this battle, a particularly important role will be played by the frontline leaders who, even while in direct command of the soldiers in the closest possible position, will often fight at their sides on the battlefield. In view of your importance as frontline commanders on the battlefield, I decided that you squad leaders should be fully acquainted with the essentials of our future plan of operations."

As he approached the end of his remarks, the commanding officer's tone took on a warmth that had previously been missing, which he communicated to Nakamura and the semicircle of other squad leaders around him.

When the commanding officer had concluded his talk, Nakamura felt a fierce surge of emotion inside him. If, as the commanding officer said, a high-ranking officer of his rank had never before directly informed low-ranking commanders like squad leaders of plans for future operations, it was true of Nakamura, too, that during the four years of military life between first entering the army as a soldier on active duty and becoming a squad leader, he had never once had this experience. Nakamura felt a trust in this commanding officer that made him realize that he would fight, that he could fight, to the bitter end, as long as it was with this "warrior." The fact that the commanding officer had informed the squad leaders in detail about future strategy was a sign of how much he trusted them. They, for their part, trusted a commanding officer who so greatly trusted them. This might not be true of all squad leaders, but it was unquestionably Nakamura's reaction. The mutual trust between the commanding officer and Squad Leader Nakamura overlapped each other. This gave him a good feeling. As long as it was with this "warrior," he would fight to the end; they could go to death together. Nakamura thought, this was what a *gyokusai* was—it was not a dog's death. This was the meaning of *gyokusai* in the true sense of the word. Yes, he could believe it. Warmth flooded his whole body.

There was one other important matter in the commanding officer's instructions. He clarified the place within the framework of future defensive operations on the island of the positions that the men had been digging and building up to now. This digging and building was definitely not the same thing as what a construction gang might do, nor were the men digging their own graves. The construction work was absolutely indispensable to future operations. More than anyone else present, Nakamura wanted to pass on this fact to the men of his command whom he had harshly rebuked and had given stinging slaps in the face when, after grinding their teeth in pain, they had occasionally complained.

The next morning, as soon as everybody was inside the cave to start working, Nakamura assembled the whole squad and had them form a semicircle around him, as the commanding officer had done the previous day. He passed on the main points of the commanding officer's instructions, emphasizing how important it was to dig holes. The main points he passed on were the four that Corporal Kon had summarized—dig, hide, stay alive, fight. But the most important goal of all had been missing—to win the fight.

5

Digging holes was hard on Nakamura too. One might say it was twice as hard on him as on anybody else because of his reputation of being a Momotarō-san squad leader who always set the pace for the others (he had been given the nickname for this reason too).

But he didn't complain. There was his sense of responsibility as squad leader, but above all, for him it was a test. It was a test of his determination to "make himself a bulwark of the Pacific Ocean," a test of his endurance in which he must succeed. The Imperial Land over which His Majesty the Emperor graciously ruled, the Land of the Gods, Japan, was now in danger. This feeling was linked to the feelings he had for his parents, his older sister, and his younger brother in the land of his ancestors whom he must protect by becoming a bulwark. Nakamura endured the hardships. The palms of his hands were covered with blisters from the pickax he swung against the hard stone walls of the caves. The blisters broke, staining his hands with blood, and falling rocks bruised his legs. The heat and the exhaustion had caused him to stop sweating completely, and finally, he was tormented for days with a fever. Despite such experiences, Nakamura never complained, not even to himself. He believed that this was his way of sacrificing himself for his fatherland, Japan, in its hour of danger.

When he stopped to think of it, he had lived this way his whole life up to the present, when he was twenty-four years old. At the thought, Nakamura was more able than ever to endure the test.

He was born the third son of a farmer who, though he owned his own land, was not particularly prosperous, and

Nakamura grew up in a village where a dry wind blew incessantly and where he was the headstrong little boss of the neighboring kids. When they played war, he was always the captain, the leader of the pack. After graduating from elementary and higher elementary school, he went to work in the village office. At night he attended a young men's training school, at the same time studying on his own a middle-school correspondence course. His efforts were rewarded when he passed the entrance examination to a technical school. Even now, he could recall how desperately he had studied until late at night, pouring icy water over his head, even when it was bitter cold, to stave off sleepiness.

Four years ago he had joined the army as a soldier on active duty. Ever since the Russo-Japanese War, the local division had been famous for its traditions of bravery and daring. Nakamura was immediately selected for duty at a post in northern Manchuria, and leaving behind his native place and his country, he headed for the region of severe cold where the intense training began for which the post was notorious. In winter it was bitterly cold, and more than ten feet of snow lay on the ground. In summer, conversely, the intense training took place in the blazing heat of the continental climate. Nakamura was equal to these tests. He combined inborn robust health with a dogged persistence of spirit twice that of the average man. He was adroit at handling a bayonet, and he was such a conspicuously model soldier that he was promoted sooner than other soldiers who had joined the army in the same year. No sooner was he promoted to sergeant than he was appointed as a squad leader. Three months later, the order was issued sending the division to the south. Nakamura, like his young buddies and the men of his command, burned with the spirit of "smite and subdue the enemy!" Although they had not had any real experience of warfare apart from having been mobilized occasionally for bandit-suppression campaigns, they shared their pride as military men in having at last obtained a place to die. They would fight side by side, and shouting "Long Live His Majesty, the Emperor!" they would die splendidly as soldiers of the Imperial Army, with nothing to be ashamed of, and would meet again at the Yasukuni Shrine, sacred to the war dead. This exalted elevation of the spirit was unquestionably shared by each and every one of them.

Their first taste of actual warfare, or rather their first encounter with its cruel remains, came when their ship managed at last to reach the main island of the Palau group after a voyage that lasted a month and had been filled with fear of enemy air attacks and torpedo attacks from submarines. The ship had even been forced to turn back in order to evade an approaching enemy task force. The capital, at the southern end of the main island, had long flourished as the administrative and developmental center of the mandated territories of the Japanese Empire in the South Pacific. The soldiers had heard that this small city was shaded by palm trees, with rows of shops, attractive in their own way, that were just as or even more prosperous as those in Japan. There were restaurants and drinking places, and plenty of women. That was what they expected, but the first thing they saw, here and there on the beach, were capsized transports lying in unsightly fashion on their sides, exposing their bottoms, and sunken warships in the harbor, visible only above the waterline. And when they disembarked from the ships, the wreckage of the town greeted them. It had been devastated by the

the breaking jewel

attacks of carrier-based planes from the enemy task force, which a month earlier had inflicted the damage on the ships anchored in the harbor. The town, burned to the ground, had been turned into heaps of rubble and reddish brown ruins.

While waiting for the landing craft that would take them to their destination, Nakamura, making some excuse, took a walk through the town. Nothing was left standing along the streets except some air-raid shelters with burned tin roofs and two or three buildings whose interiors had been gutted by flames. As Nakamura continued walking, he found himself before a Shinto shrine on a hilltop outside the town. It had survived completely unscathed. The shrine had been erected here, at the heart of the Japanese-administered territories of the South Pacific, to pray for the preservation of order and security in the region. Nakamura had been told by a member of the transport crew that the big *torii* gate and the shrine's hall of worship had been built with wood from the ironwood, a tree that grows only in the South Pacific. Its wood, he said, was as hard as the name suggested. The crew member, a man older than himself, had served before the war aboard ships on the South Seas run. He urged Nakamura to pay a visit. "The shrine's quite a place. You should go there and pray for success in the fighting." And now Nakamura, without having intended it, had found his way to the shrine quite by accident. He felt it was a good sign. He entered the deserted precincts of the shrine. Bougainvillea, which he saw for the first time, was blooming profusely, and in the distance, the perfectly clear blue sea beyond the coral reef stretched peacefully. He entered the precincts of the shrine. Not a soul was in sight. When he clapped his hands twice in prayer before the shrine built of ironwood, the sound reverberated loudly. He prayed for the prosperity of the Imperial Throne, the safety of the fatherland, and the success of the Japanese Southern Expeditionary Army, in that order.

Just as he was about to leave the shrine, passing under the ironwood *torii*, an old woman, her kimono and her elegantly held parasol looking quite out of place, came up from one side, as if she had been waiting for him to reach the spot. She called to him as she approached, "You're a soldier from Manchuria, aren't you?" Nakamura nodded, whereupon she politely bowed and said, "Thank you for all your trouble." Then, with an air of hesitation, she added falteringly, "There's something I'd like to ask you . . ."

The question asked by this dignified-looking woman, who was as old as Nakamura's mother back home, took him by surprise: "What is going to happen to Japan now?" When Nakamura failed to answer, she went on, "It wasn't so long ago, but any number of big warships of the Joint Fleet came into the harbor, and we were all so happy, thinking that everything would be all right, that we had nothing to worry about. A great many sailors came ashore, and the town became quite lively. Then suddenly they all went away, and the next thing we knew, the air raids started, and the whole town went up in smoke. Wasn't that the same thing as if the Joint Fleet had run away without fighting? Then, a little later on, the commander in chief left here by plane only to get killed in an accident. What is going to happen to Japan now?" The woman delivered all this in one breath, as if pouring out everything she had stored up in her heart, then gave a great sigh. Lowering her voice, as if afraid her words might be overheard, she added, "They say the enemy will be landing here any day."

the breaking jewel

Her stories of both the Joint Fleet's abandoning the island and the commander in chief's being killed in an accident came as news to Nakamura, who, during the move from northern Manchuria to this island, had not been in touch with developments in the outside world; but he answered slowly, emphasizing his words, "Japan is the Land of the Gods. We'll win, no matter what." This was how he answered the woman's question "What is going to happen to Japan now?" He started to follow this with "It's because we're convinced of this that we've come all this distance so we might make of ourselves 'bulwarks of the Pacific Ocean,'" but he confusedly swallowed his words, as the fact occurred to him that this island itself was already a bulwark.

The woman, whose height came up only to Nakamura's shoulders, asked, looking up at his face, "I wonder if you'd mind taking this with you?"

She seemed extremely hesitant, but she put in Nakamura's hands a small parcel wrapped in newspaper. He looked at her with a dubious expression on his face. He opened the package, as she suggested. A piece of cloth fell out. It was a "thousand-stitch belt."

Her son, while on business in Kyushu, had been drafted and assigned to the division from the part of country where he was legally domiciled and from there had been sent to the front in central China. She had made this thousand-stitch belt and planned to send it to him, but the mail service from the island to the mainland had by now been interrupted.

The woman rambled on. While she was wondering what to do, she heard rumors that troops were coming to the island from northern Manchuria, and this gave her a good idea. Her house and shop had been burned in the attacks by carrier planes, and she had taken refuge in the house of an acquaintance near the shrine. But she felt sure that some of the soldiers in the reinforcement army from northern Manchuria would come to worship at the shrine, and there was likely to be one about the same age as her son. If she gave the thousand-stitch belt to this soldier, she felt sure that the belt would protect him, and it would also protect her own son. So thinking or, rather, so believing, she had been coming to the shrine once every day with the paper package containing the thousand-stitch belt. "And you . . ." she began falteringly, "How old would you be?" She was in tears, embarrassed to ask the question. Nakamura told her, and she responded, "One year older than my son." For a moment she looked intently up at Nakamura's face, her expression tense. She asked, "Would you really be willing to take this thousand-stitch belt?" The tone of her voice suggested she would not take no for an answer. There was that much strength in her voice.

"I accept it gratefully." Nakamura replied, as if overpowered by the strength behind her words. Taking the paper package in his hands, he lifted it reverently to the level of his eyes

He had not in the least anticipated this movement of his hands, but at that moment nothing could have been more natural. It was if he was accepting from his mother back at home the thousand-stitch belt into which she had put all her love. Nakamura, feeling this, was moved to tears.

Nakamura's first experience of actual warfare, as opposed to the wreckage left by war, came barely six hours after he had accepted a thousand-stitch belt from an unknown woman.

The distance in a straight line from the main island to the small island where his outfit was to be stationed was forty kilometers. The large-size landing crafts, empty weight nine and a half tons, had a speed of eight knots, and were operated by "land sailors" of the marine transport units. Nakamura heard that many of them had formerly worked on fishing boats or on motor-powered sailing boats. Nakamura estimated that it would take four hours to reach the small island, but perhaps because of the excessive weight load—the landing craft was carrying easily twice the normal seventy passengers, all fully armed soldiers—or perhaps because it was simply not possible to travel quickly through the channel that had been opened in the coral reef with its many shallows, it was six hours before they finally reached their destination, a rudely made pier at the northern tip of the small island.

These were six hours of unremitting fear—enemy planes might attack at any moment, or they might be torpedoed by a submarine. If this had been peacetime, the hours they spent on the water, eyes fixed on the small island ahead, coral atolls in the sea on both sides, would surely have been exhilarating, but all that Nakamura and the others crouched in the hold of the landing barge could see were one another's faces bearing up under their fear. They listened in silence as a reservist, Private First Class Ishizaki, who before being called up had worked as a clerk at a hotel in Atami or some such hot spring resort—that was his story, though some said that in fact he had been nothing more than a barker soliciting customers—babbled on about how, when the war ended, assuming he was still alive, he wanted to try his luck at opening a combination restaurant and hotel in a town somewhere in the South Seas, like the town they had just left behind—in fact, he fully intended to. The special attraction of his future hotel would be fishing boats that would take guests out into the coral sea where they were now or, it might be even better to have pleasure launches. He promised to invite them all. The others all listened in silence as he chattered on. He seemed unlikely ever to stop until finally somebody, even before Nakamura could intervene, called out, "Come off it. Calm down."

Ishizaki's talkativeness probably revealed just how frightened he was. He no doubt had reached the point that his nerves could take no more unless he kept rattling on about such silly things. Nakamura endured his fear in silence. But in his case, it was not simply that he was afraid to die. This fear was linked to the feeling that if he died here on the water, it would be a dog's death and nothing more. He had had this feeling while on the transport, and it had mounted all but unbearably in the hold of the landing barge, where the possibility of dying a dog's death was all the greater. This was a sign that his fear had also mounted.

After the six-hour test of endurance, shouts of "Arrival. Make ready to go ashore" at last came from the "land sailors." Their hoarse voices sounded to Nakamura like voices from heaven. But on the heels of these voices from heaven, just as they were about to leave the landing barge and take their first steps on the small island that was their destination, roars of hell suddenly erupted from the skies behind them. A cluster of carrier planes, apparently having detected the wake left by the landing barges on their way from the main island here, had descended on them. In an instant, a clatter of machine-gun strafing from Grumman carrier planes began, along with the thud of small bombs dropped by the planes as they strafed. The next instant, some in the line of soldiers who had hastily thrown themselves flat on the ground were already dying. Among the men covered with blood and screaming in the agony of death was the reservist, formerly the clerk of a hotel or possibly a barker, who a little earlier had rambled on interminably about his dreams of opening a combination restaurant and hotel in the South Seas after the war and who had invited all the others to go sightseeing aboard his pleasure launch. As a matter of fact, he did not raise any death cry. And, of course, he did not shout "Long Live the Emperor" either. He died instantly, without uttering a word.

Private First Class Ishizaki was the first member of Nakamura's squad to be killed in action. Who would be the second, the third, the fourth? Nakamura's thoughts ran on as he walked, accompanying the body on a stretcher. He recalled an expression taught him by a soldier of the garrison on the main island—"the one-tenth that saves your life." The man had prefaced his explanation of the phrase by describing how popular it had become among the soldiers of the garrison. It meant that if the aim of the enemy's gun was one-tenth off, or if there was an error of one-tenth in the bombsight of an enemy plane, you would be safe, even if your pal standing next to you was hit by a bullet or a bomb. When the elderly soldier informed him of the phrase, Nakamura had thought, "Of all the stupid things to say!" but there was truth in it. Brushing off the thought, Nakamura said to himself in tones of rage, "First Class Private Ishizaki, I, your squad leader, promise you I will, without fail, avenge your death by killing twice as many or three times as many American devils for each man we lose."

6

After receiving the commanding officer's instructions, Nakamura threw himself into his work with even greater zeal than before, whether it consisted of rehearsals of interception tactics, repeated day after day and night after night, or of going into the caves to construct retrenchments. The doubts that up until now had remained, deep in his heart, were gone. The determination to make of himself a bulwark in the Pacific was now firmly linked to winning the war. Digging holes for positions was no less firmly linked to the same objective. By digging now in the caves, they were constructing a "bulwark of the Pacific" that would bring victory. Nakamura was steadily forging a link connecting these activities in a straight line to the goal, victory. He was clearly aware of what he was doing and saw himself in these terms. Greater strength than ever before flowed into the hands gripping a pickax.

After he had passed on to them the commanding officer's instructions, the men of his squad also put everything they had into both the drills and the construction work. They had visibly changed. Kon, the noncommissioned officer attached to the squad, said so to Nakamura. "Squad leader, all hands are raring now to do their best." Kon sometimes spoke of members of the squad as "hands," using the old-fashioned locution for humorous effect. "Think that'll be enough for us to win?" Nakamura responded. Kon did not answer. He merely smiled.

Kon, like Nakamura, was the kind of man who never grumbled. There were any number of other men in Nakamura's squad who did not complain, but Kon differed from them categorically. They gave the impression of clenching their teeth and bearing up, but nothing in Kon suggested such feelings. Then the question was, what about Nakamura himself? That was something he himself didn't understand. He brushed aside all questions relating to himself.

Of course, Kon was no superman. Obviously, like everybody else, he found the drills and the construction work exhausting. It was exhausting, but he bore up. The impression of "bearing up" held true whatever he did. Somewhere in the way he bore up one sensed extra reserves. No, "extra reserves" is probably not the right expression. He looked at life, keeping it at arm's length, and thought, "That's what life is like, and it won't do any good to make a big fuss over it." Some such belief, reflected in the attitudes and actions of his daily life, was probably what gave people the impression he had extra reserves. He couldn't properly remember even the Imperial Rescript to Soldiers and Sailors, the basic spiritual guide—or so considered—for the fighting men of the empire. This was at once apparent from the haphazard answers with which he managed to scrape by when the company commander, a fault-finding graduate of the military academy and a stickler for trivialities, obliged on occasion even noncommissioned officers like Nakamura and Kon to recite from memory the Imperial Rescript. Kon was by no means slipshod in performing drills or fatigue duty, but unlike Nakamura, he was never one to take the initiative and lead the way. All the same, his skill with the bayonet, on a level with Nakamura's, ranked as best in the regiment. (When there were bayonet meets held at the post in northern Manchuria, sometimes Nakamura was in first place, only for Kon to win the next tournament.) When it came to marksmanship, Kon was probably the best shot, not merely in the regiment, but in the whole division. Once, at the range in northern Manchuria, riflemen selected from each section of the division were required to shoot (in place of the usual targets) a herd of roe deer scurrying through the fields. Kon acquired a reputation as the only man to score direct hits on this most difficult of moving targets, felling not one but two deer.

There was another famous story told about him. The authenticity of the story cannot be vouched for, but it is said that when Kon was being hazed as a recruit, he was unable to recite by heart the section on rifles in the infantry manual. As a consequence, it seems, he was soundly slapped. The text contains such passages as "To assume a position of prone firing, keep your head faced in the direction of the target, and with your left hand, slide open the ammunition pouch to left and right, advancing your left foot about half a pace in front of the right foot, at the same time turning the upper part of your body halfway to the right; then hit the ground with your right knee, and holding your left arm before you, lower it to the ground. Then, with your body faced in the direction of the firing, drop down to an angle of approximately thirty degrees, at the same time extending your gun with your right hand, and with your left hand . . ."

Kon defiantly told the noncommissioned officer administering the drill that although he was unable to recite the words by heart, he could perform the actions perfectly, exactly as stipulated. Naturally, this earned him another slap, but a veteran soldier, observing what was going on, said in amusement, "Well then, let's see you do it," adding the threat, "If you can't, I'll knock you for a loop." Kon remained unperturbed. "Yes, sir," he replied, and at once flawlessly performed before the noncommissioned officers the actions of firing from prone position. The story ends happily with the drill instructor and the difficult veteran soldier unable to find anything to criticize in Kon's "model performance" of firing from a prone position. Another "legend" carries the story a bit further. According to this legend, after completing his "model performance," Kon revealed that the section in the infantry manual had been written after observing his movements, but the epilogue is a bit too perfect. All one can say definitely is that the "legend" proves that from the time he was a recruit, Kon was an extremely good shot.

When people praised his shooting, Kon would reply in embarrassment, "I guess I was just born to be a soldier," shaking a head that, in his own words, was twice the normal size, so big he had never found a regulation cap, fatigue cap, or helmet to fit it, no matter how many he tried on. He added, "Some people are born to be scholars, to sit at a desk and study; others are good at throwing a baseball. The man who's suited to study should become a scholar and get a job at a college somewhere. The man who's good at throwing a baseball can become a professional player. It's the same thing for soldiering."

But "soldiering" was not the only thing for which Kon was suited. When it came to building positions and digging holes, his handling of a pickax was masterly. Whether they were field positions on the coastal reef or retrenchments in a cave somewhere in the middle of the island, when Kon struck a precisely aimed blow at hard bedrock or rock face, it would split beautifully. Moreover, unlike Nakamura, the palms of his hands had never become red with blood, no matter how much he wielded his pickax. When praised for his handling of the pickax, he did not say, "I guess I was just born to be a construction worker." All he said was, "I've done all kinds of things in my life." At such times there was no trace of embarrassment on his face. His expression was in fact severer than usual.

Kon was popular with the other soldiers. His popularity, it might be said, went beyond the squad or company level. It stemmed, first of all, from his being an excellent soldier, a man who by temperament was born for "soldiering." He was undoubtedly a model soldier in the sense that he excelled at his profession, but he was definitely not a model soldier in the same sense that Nakamura was one. A man like Kon is a kind of "hero of the crossroads"—a folk hero—and, as such, enjoys popularity among the masses. In a military organization the "masses" are the lower ranks, and that probably accounts for Kon's popularity among the ordinary soldiers. Nakamura certainly was not an unpopular noncommissioned officer, but the popularity of a model soldier among model soldiers did not approach the popularity of a folk hero.

As is often true of "folk heroes" of the crossroads in their associations with the masses, Kon was kind to the lower ranks and often helped them. At other times he could be merciless in the brutal slaps he dealt his subordinates, but it was also he who, like a father, patiently instructed clumsy recruits, hitherto subjected to nothing but beatings, in the knack of firing a gun. When some blockhead lost a rifle part and was desperate what to do, Kon would swipe a part from somewhere to make up the count; for that soldier, he definitely was a "folk hero."

Or Kon might, giving the blockhead special treatment, accompany him to the barrack square in search of the missing part and, in the end, find it. Even at such times he was indifferent to praise and, with an embarrassed look on his face, would say, "It's like somebody who's naturally good at climbing trees helping another guy who's clumsy at it."

It wasn't simply that he was kind to the soldiers. When they judge it is safe to do so, soldiers are likely to speak ill of their superior officers. Kon seems not to have actively sought to join the circles of gripers, but every once in a while he would come out with something that was both caustic and accurate, and this also won him popularity. Nakamura did not know what was being said about himself and had no intention of finding out, but the man most often the butt of subordinates' criticism was the company commander, a graduate of officer candidates' school known by the nickname "Captain Centipede." Among officers with his background, men who have been commissioned after first graduating from an ordinary university and then from an officer candidates' school, there are some who try to overcome their real or imagined inferiority in the world of the military to officers of the regular army, graduates of the military academy, by acting more officer-like than they, blustering and asserting their authority before subordinates. Nakamura had heard Kon's opinion of this "Captain Centipede": "The captain is a perfect officer. He's stuck-up and he's incompetent." This not only was an accurate description of "Captain Centipede" but also was directed at officers in general.

Kon had a wide range of connections. He contrived to obtain somewhere special ration cigarettes that he brought back to the squad and divided up among the men. He also brought them papayas and mangoes, delicacies of the South Seas that Nakamura and the other men had never before tasted. When

Nakamura asked how he got them, Kon said he had received them from people of the island. Nakamura was aware that natives who had formerly been employed in building the naval base were now being used as coolies to construct fortifications. He had caught sight of them a couple of times slowly carrying dirt and stones in straw baskets. But it was only when he asked Kon where he got the fruit and Kon told him they came from the islanders that he realized for the first time that there were also natives living somewhere on the island. Kon went to their houses, and they gave him the fruit. No, Kon corrected himself, it was actually barter. Nakamura asked in surprise, "You mean there are people you know among them?" "That's right," replied Kon, eating a mango with evident relish. "Any number of them." Kon in turn looked dubiously at Nakamura. "It's their island we're living on, right?"

Nakamura was grateful for the special cigarettes, the papayas, and the mangoes, but he appreciated most the information of every kind that Kon brought back from his wide range of acquaintances. The information extended in many directions, from training, work schedules, and personnel changes within the outfit to strategic plans for the entire division and even the general war situation. Kon would always start off with, "Squad leader, I wonder if you've heard this story?" Then in a low voice, as if talking to himself, he would rate the news he brought: "This one's 100 percent sure," "This is 70 percent."

In March the news Kon brought that the Joint Fleet, which had "evacuated" the main island, had recently suffered a severe defeat was rated as "70 percent" when he first informed Nakamura. This became "80 percent," "90 percent," and finally "100 percent." As the news became more and more reliable, it also became more precise and more tragic, or even desperate, with details of how many Japanese aircraft carriers had been sunk, how many hundreds of planes (not enemy but Japanese planes) had been shot down. Kon was friendly with a noncommissioned officer at headquarters, a man who had lived as a child in Hawaii and who was in charge of gathering intelligence from intercepted enemy radio broadcasts. Even when Nakamura rebuked Kon, asking, "You mean to say you can believe stories coming from the enemy?" he showed no sign of budging: "In matters of this kind, Mr. Enemy doesn't make mistakes." The words had something of the detached attitude of "You're free to believe it or not believe it, whichever you please."

"I wonder if you know, Squad Leader, what Mr. Enemy calls *gyokusai?*" This was something else, Kon informed him, he had learned from the man who had grown up in Hawaii. "I was told they call it a suicide attack or else a banzai charge." Kon, looking at Nakamura's face, asked teasingly, "Squad leader, which of the two do you think is the better translation?" When Nakamura failed to reply, Kon answered his own question, "I don't like either one." He added, "That's because I don't feel like committing suicide, and I have no intention of crying banzai when I die. I'm going to win, that's all. That's what I plan." The words repeated what he had said not long before.

Four or five days after the commanding officer issued his directive on the proposed site in a cave of the underground command post, Kon brought a new report. The army brass had apparently sent word to the garrisons of each island that the plan of defensive strategy for the islands had been fundamentally changed: "When the American forces storm ashore, they will be supported by such overwhelmingly strong fire-power that it will no longer be possible to annihilate them at the water's edge. Shift immediately to a war of attrition, making use of depth positions to the rear, and hold out to the last soldier. Strengthen your retrenchments so as to make possible this in-depth strategy."

Nakamura interrupted Kon's story to ask, "Isn't that just what the commanding officer informed us the other day?"

"That's right," Kon nodded. The problem was that the completed retrenchments were still far from sufficient. "And," he continued, "there's no telling when the fortifications will be completed or even if we'll ever be able to complete the kind of strong fortifications they want." He glanced at the mouth of the cave where they had been working for some days, not the same one where Nakamura not long ago had passed on instructions from the commanding officer.

There was another problem. Speaking as if in response to Kon's words, Nakamura declared that the vital question was *when* the Americans would land. Even as he spoke, he kept looking from the mouth of the cave to Kon. Kon slowly shook his head. It was so big it was always extremely difficult to find a cap or helmet to fit it.

 7

Kon was a Korean. No, it would be more exact to say he was a Japanese from the peninsula. Just as a part of Japan is known as "Osaka Prefecture," and other parts as "Okayama Prefecture" or Hokkaido, there was an area known as "the Korean peninsula." If some ignoramus looked dubious when Kon identified himself as "a Japanese from the peninsula," he would carefully explain that if you said of somebody that he was an Osaka man or an Okayama man, it wasn't exactly the same as calling him a Japanese, but of course that was implied. In the same way, he was a "peninsula man," a Japanese from the Korean peninsula. This was the explanation he offered everyone, superior officers and subordinates alike. His trump card was the assertion: "I'm soldier in the Imperial Army. Could anyone who's not a Japanese be a soldier in the Imperial Army?"

He would go on, "I volunteered under the Special Volunteer System and became a soldier of the Imperial Army. I wasn't the only one. Thousands and even tens of thousands of peninsula men did the same. As a matter of fact, they've now introduced conscription on the Korean peninsula, and young men from the peninsula are now doing a splendid job, performing their duties as members of the Imperial Army and Navy and as Japanese." Sometimes Kon spoke about Governor-General Minami. As a convinced advocate of the "union of the home provinces and Korea," the governor-general had initiated the Special Volunteer System. He had even ordered peninsula men to thrash any Japanese who said anything to the effect that people from the peninsula were not Japanese. Kon would often say, "At the national elementary schools on the peninsula, the children all swear an oath of allegiance. That's to prove they're subjects of the Japanese Empire." He would ask with an expression of puzzlement on his face why children at national elementary schools in the home provinces were not required to do the same.

When asked the question by a Japanese from the peninsula, a Japanese soldier in the Imperial Army like himself, Nakamura also found it strange. He started to say that the oath of allegiance was intended to make people from the peninsula into worthy subjects of the empire, only to stop, foreseeing he was likely to be asked in return, "Then, are all Japanese worthy subjects of the empire?"

Nakamura did not really know why Kon had volunteered and become an army special volunteer. Nor did he know for what reason and under what circumstances Kon had been assigned to Nakamura's division, at a time when the division was stationed at a post in northern Manchuria, a division that had no connection whatsoever with peninsula people. At present, just as Kon had said, any number of peninsula men were being taken into the army as conscripts. This surely would occasion many problems. Nakamura had heard that by way of preparation for this problem, "peninsula soldiers," men who like Kon had volunteered, were being assigned to each division to guide the conscripts. But Nakamura wasn't even sure that Kon was a Korean or, rather, a peninsula man. About all that Nakamura definitely knew about him beforehand was that Kon was a year his senior in the service, a soldier who had eaten Imperial Army chow for more than a year longer than himself; Kon was therefore a senior comrade to whom he automatically owed respect. (Both Kon and Nakamura were well aware of the rule in the military that, quite apart from "public" seniority that depends on rank, "private" seniority, determined by the number of years in the service, also had to be respected. The language they used to each other followed this rule. Kon "publicly" called Nakamura "Mr. Squad Leader," and his language was suitably deferential, but in "private" conversation he spoke much more familiarly, calling him simply "Squad Leader." Nakamura, in the same way, on public occasions invariably called him Corporal Kon, as one of his subordinates, but, less formal in private, called him Mr. Kon.) Nakamura could guess how much hardship it had cost Kon to rise to the rank of corporal from the time he entered the Imperial Army. No doubt it had been harder for him than for an "ordinary" Japanese, but Nakamura had almost no information on the subject and had no intention of learning at this late date. One thing he was sure of and could remember quite distinctly was that one day while he was at the post in northern Manchuria—the same day he was promoted to sergeant and was simultaneously appointed as a squad leader, an unusually rapid promotion—a noncommissioned officer with a head twice the normal size had suddenly appeared and introduced himself with a bare minimum of words: "Corporal Kon, reporting for duty. I have been appointed as a noncommissioned officer on temporary duty with your squad." From then on, he and Nakamura had lived together in the squad and gradually, both publicly and privately, had become friendly. Before long, they both were ordered to the South Pacific and had come to this island. They did not know when the Americans would land, but the day of the attack was definitely getting closer, and "making their bodies into bulwarks of the Pacific Ocean," they were about to engage in a life-and-death struggle against the American invaders.

The first time he met anyone, Kon would emphasize that his name was to be read that way, not as Kin or Kim. He would point out that even among Japanese from the home provinces, any number, from ancient times on, had read their names as Kon, and it was true of him too. Quite apart from family names, the character was read as *kon* rather than *kin* in the name of the Kondō [Golden Hall] of the Hōryūji temple and the title of Ozaki Kōyō's novel *Konjiki yasha* [*The Demon Gold*]. He managed in this way to be called Corporal Kon, and if anyone called him Kin, he would invariably correct that person, "My name is Kon." He would punctiliously correct even superior officers with a "The name is Corporal Kon, sir." At times, listening to Kon correct someone, Nakamura found his insistence irritating, and he was tempted to blurt out, "What difference does it make how your name is pronounced?" But regardless of the occasion, Kon invariably made the correction. It was Kon himself who unthinkingly informed Nakamura, who knew nothing of such matters, that on the peninsula some years back, a "changing of family and personal names" had been put into effect. People with the surname Yi became Iwamoto, Kim became Kanayama, Pak became Arai, and so on, replacing Korean with Japanese names. After finishing this account, Kon added, "It had nothing to do with me. That's because my family name is Kon, and there also are Japanese with the same name." It may have been in order to make this final comment that Kon had brought up the matter of how Korean names had been changed.

Nakamura once asked Kon where in the peninsula he came from. Kon answered, Keijō, then explained that formerly it was known as Seoul. "Even now there are still plenty of peninsula people who call it by that name," he said, informing Nakamura of something else he did not know. Nakamura was struck dumb with surprise, not simply because this was the first time in his life he had ever heard a word of Korean, but because the unfamiliar language had issued from the mouth of someone who looked exactly like a Japanese, who pronounced Japanese correctly and did not say *pogu* instead of *boku* for "I," and who, a soldier of the Imperial Army, always referred to himself as a Japanese from the peninsula.

Kon repeated the name Seoul: "Peninsula people say Seoul instead of Keijō." Nakamura was incapable of pronouncing the sound. It reverberated in his ears, strange but appealing. Two or three others—men in Nakamura's squad—were listening nearby. They stared in silence, as if intimidated, at Corporal Kon's mouth as he pronounced the unfamiliar place-name. No doubt it was a totally new experience for them too.

Just the other day Kon had suddenly asked Nakamura, "Squad leader, I wonder if you know a guy called Nakamura-san?" Kon's tone somehow suggested to Nakamura he was being teased, and he guessed from the start that the question was leading up to something. "Never heard of him," Nakamura answered, a solemn look on his face. Kon explained that "Nakamura-san" was what peninsula people called a Japanese blowhard, a one-dimensional four-flusher. Probably in the past there had actually been such a Japanese of that name in Korea. As he explained, Kon looked at Nakamura's face as if to make sure of his reactions. Nakamura returned the question, "You mean I'm a Nakamura-san?" Kon shook his head exaggeratedly. "No, Mr. Squad Leader, you are certainly Mr. Nakamura, but you're not a Nakamura-san. You're serious, you have depth. You're the exact opposite of a Nakamura-san. But in the fighting ahead of us, I wonder if you'll be able to keep going if all you do is act as an exact opposite. I mean, if you intend to go on living, if you intend to go on living and fighting." Kon pressed Nakamura for an answer, continuing to look at his face. He did not add, "if you intend to win." This was something of which Nakamura himself was aware. "Thanks for the tip," he replied. "I won't become a Nakamura-san. I'll stick it out to the end as Nakamura." Nakamura said this to conclude the conversation, making a clear distinction between Nakamura and a Nakamura-san.

 8

Enemy air raids became fiercer by the day, and the situation as a whole became increasingly tense. The intervals between air raids had shortened, and the scale was expanded. First, B-17 bombers would drop one-ton bombs, brutally blasting away the dense growth of trees in the jungle and opening up huge holes everywhere. Then Grumman fighters would follow on their tails, dropping small bombs wherever there were signs of life, quick to shower down machinegun strafing. This combined operation by the enemy of land-based bombers and carrier-based planes grew bigger and more skillful by the day. There were almost no counterattacks by the garrison. The treasured Zero fighter planes remained hidden in the jungle and did not leave the ground. In order to preserve the secrecy of the sites of installations and to conserve ammunition for future intercepting tactics, antiaircraft fire was not raised except under the most exceptional circumstances. The watchword was to keep out of sight now and wait for the decisive battle. Nakamura repeated this over and over to his men who, in their foxholes, listened with frustration to the roar from the sky, the explosion of bombs, and the sounds of machine-gun strafing, the proof of the dominance of the enemy planes. It was not only to his men that he repeated this injunction. He repeated it to himself as well. Any number of the soldiers had fallen victim to the domineering enemy. Fortunately, there had been no victims in Nakamura's squad, but five men in the company had already been killed. Even the company commander had been slightly wounded by shrapnel from a bomb dropped by a Grumman fighter. With one arm in a white sling, he would walk around, visiting each squad, finding fault as usual, but a good thing happened: because of his wound, Commander Centipede was assigned to force headquarters, and a first lieutenant, a graduate of the military academy whom Nakamura had known well ever since they were together at the post in northern Manchuria, was appointed as the new company commander. He was young but had steady nerves and carried himself with the dignity of a fully grown man. Perhaps force headquarters, well aware that his men had no confidence in Commander Centipede, had been waiting for an opportunity to replace him. Another good thing that resulted from Commander Centipede's wound was that because the young lieutenant enjoyed the trust of the force commander and was considered to be one of the finest officers in the outfit, no sooner was he appointed as the new company commander than the company was designated as the main force in the planned strategy of annihilating the Americans at the water's edge as soon as they came ashore. The company commander told the squad leaders, and they informed the men: "We've been given as the place we're to die the most important spot. It's a great honor.

We'll fight to the death. We must fight." The men—including those in Nakamura's squad—broke into a roar of war cries. Or as Corporal Kon put it, "All hands are chomping at the bit for a fight."

Unless they were prepared to fight, every one of them would simply die, killed by the Americans. They would have to fight even to stay alive. The result would be either life or death. After saying, "We've been given a place to die," Nakamura tried to put into words the thoughts that welled up in his heart, but he stopped. He had only to look at the eyes of his men to understand that they felt the same as himself. One and all, their eyes glared with rage. Nakamura was talking to them late at night in the shadows of the shore reef, during a break between bouts of the night attack drills they repeated night after night. In a night sky that was almost frighteningly clear, the moon hung; it too was frightening in its clarity. Is it to such a condition that the people are referring when they speak of the "dazzling brilliance" of the moon? The moonlight sharply illuminated the faces of each of his men, as if to remind Nakamura that he must not entertain the slightest doubt about them.

The drills were stepped up. They were using live ammunition, though hoarding it. It was no longer a question of each man killing one enemy. Each man must kill ten. If each man could, without fail, kill ten American devils, this would open up a first possibility of victory. On a more basic level, it was kill or be killed.

"The enemy will outnumber us ten to one. Unless each of you kills ten of them, you definitely will be killed. Even if their tanks come roaring at you, don't be afraid. Blaze away with your antiaircraft guns. Run at them with hand grenades.

A grenade doesn't hold much explosive, but it's powerful enough to knock out a tank. But don't charge recklessly. Don't be in a hurry to get killed. Each man who gets killed opens a hole in our ranks. Take cover. Be clever about hiding yourself. Lure the American devils to you, and when they're at close range, make every shot count. And use your bayonets. Run them through. Kill them. If you're wounded, stab them back. Kill them and die a glorious death in battle. Don't be taken alive and suffer the shame of becoming a prisoner."

The digging of holes and building of fortifications went on. The men began to carry ammunition, provisions, and water to retrenchment positions in the caves. On the island, sources of water were limited, and water storage was a major problem. Poured into containers of every description, the water was heavy as they carried it on paths between the rocks. One of these days men would go into caves all over the island, and although they would be few in number, they would fight to the last. The transport and storage of supplies to positions in the caves were carried out with this likelihood in mind. Thoughts of its future importance made the work more demanding.

Private Second Class Kaneshiro appeared in Nakamura's squad just when the men were frantically busy carrying and storing supplies. They could guess from the awkwardness in the movements of this unknown, pint-size man that he had probably been a civilian until the day before. He was wearing a cheap-looking ersatz uniform, typical of what was being made at the time. The second class private all but staggered as he made his way into the cave, coming to a halt before Nakamura. He clumsily mouthed the words he had been taught: "Squad Leader Nakamura. Private Second Class Kaneshiro begs to inform you he has just arrived and is reporting for duty." No doubt he was nervous—his lips trembled and his words shook. Nakamura at once recalled that he had received a couple of days earlier a notice from the company commander stating that recruits, called up locally on the main island, would be assigned to each squad.

"Private Second Class Kaneshiro, have you got a gun?" Nakamura without thinking asked, although he could quite plainly see that the second class private, a civilian lately mustered into the army (as he revealed by the awkward way in which he had pronounced the prescribed words), had arrived with a rifle in his hand. He asked the question because he had heard a report that because there was such a shortage even of rifles, not every one of the newly recruited thirteen hundred resident Japanese on the main island could be supplied; instead, they had been sent off to garrisons on other islands of the region armed with six-foot-long sticks of ironwood in place of rifles. When Nakamura heard that new soldiers could not be provided with rifles, the "soul of the warrior" in the old phrase, he had felt miserable that the fortunes of the Imperial Army had so declined, but this civilian turned private second class did have a rifle, even though it was an old-fashioned Model 38. A bayonet also hung from his waist. Nakamura muttered to himself without realizing it, "That's good." Private Second Class Kaneshiro looked startled, as if he had been scolded.

Kaneshiro was short, but he was solidly and powerfully built. This was evident despite the shabby, ersatz uniform he was wearing. He was thirty-one, rather old for a recruit. Nakamura looked at the documents he had brought.

"You're from Okinawa?" Kon, standing at the side, interjected.

"From Itoman, sir," the private second class replied.

Nakamura asked, "What did you do in civilian life?"

"I was a fisherman. But from some time back I'd been working as a civilian employee on a motor-powered sailboat. My job was sailboat transport, sir."

"And what happened to the job?"

"The motor-powered sailboat sank, sir. It was done in by a Grumman."

"And you were rescued? . . . Did you swim for it?" Nakamura continued his questions.

"Yes, sir, I swam. For two days. I was rescued by a destroyer that happened to be passing by."

Kon again interrupted, "You must be quite a swimmer. Not so surprising, of course, in a fisherman from Itoman." He added, "Private Second Class Kaneshiro. In case of an emergency, you may have to swim to the main island for liaison."

Private Second Class Kaneshiro again looked startled. Kon's words also came as a surprise to Nakamura, who looked at Kon's face under the big head that no ordinary combat cap could cover. Kon seemed to have something on his mind. Then he said, "My name's Kon . . . Corporal Kon. It's written with the same Kin as in your name, but it's pronounced Kon."*

Kon abruptly demanded in a loud voice, "Private Second Class Kaneshiro, are you a good shot?"

Kaneshiro answered nervously, as if intimidated by the implications of the noncommissioned officer's sudden question, "Pretty good, sir." The awkwardness in the instant-

---

*The same character (meaning "metal") is pronounced as *kane* in native pronunciation but as *kin* (or *kon*) in the Sino-Japanese pronunciation.

soldier's voice had become even more pronounced. In the same tones, with hesitance, he added, "Being a fisherman, my eyes are good."

"Well, I'm going to give you some special instructions. Are you ready? The fighting we're going to do from now on will be a battle at the water's edge for this itty-bitty island. It'll be hand-to-hand fighting for every one of us; kill or be killed. When the fighting reaches that stage, naval guns with their sixteen-inch shells are of no use, and it'll be too late also for one-ton bombs or machine-gun strafing. If they let fly with such things, we and the Yanks will be dead men together. That's why they can't use them. When the fighting reaches the final stage, the only question will be whether or not one rifle shot hits the target. Of course, if you head straight into one of those automatic rifles the Yanks carry, you won't stand a chance. I'm sorry to tell you, but the rifle they gave you is a relic of the Russo-Japanese War. You're out of luck. All the same, if you fire a hundred shots, try to make each one blow out the brains of a Yank. Make sure you kill ten of them. That will be your personal victory."

Nakamura was of the same opinion, but he felt there was something peculiar in the way Kon had shifted from his usual, somehow offhand way of talking to this sudden eloquence. He looked at Kon, but there was no change in his expression.

Kon went on, "In hand-to-hand fighting, each soldier is on his own. Each and every man fights on his own. Nobody can help you—not your pals or anybody else. This means the war is really each man's individual war. It doesn't matter how many of them come at you or how superior they may be materially. When it gets to this point, it's a war between one man and another. No matter how few men you've got on your side or how short you are of supplies, if you, you alone, are strong, you're one man, and your enemy is also one man, right? You can do pretty well. No matter how powerful the country the other guy belongs to, when you're on your own, you can fight on equal terms. You can knock the other guy flat. That's what I think. And that's why I intend to fight my own personal war. To fight and win."

Kon kept his voice low, exactly as if he were talking to himself. For a moment he seemed to have broken off, only to resume immediately, this time in a strong voice.

"Do you follow me? Private Second Class Kaneshiro, I'm giving you a good education. I shouldn't be saying this about myself, but I'm the best shot in the force. Now that I've trained you with these special instructions, you can, even with your old Model 38 rifle, do better at blowing out the enemy's brains than guys with Model 99s. You can kill ten of them, all by yourself."

It seemed as if Kon would never stop talking. Nakamura, choosing an opportune moment, said in a loud voice that was like an order, "Private Second Class Kaneshiro, you may go." If he hadn't done so, Kon might really have kept talking forever.

Two or three days after this incident, Kon went up to Nakamura saying, "Squad Leader, do you know what that fisherman from Itoman was wearing under his shirt?" By way of an answer, Nakamura asked first what effects Kon's special instructions had had on Private Second Class Kaneshiro. Kon's answer was brief: "He's the real thing." For a while afterward, Kon talked about the fisherman–private second class. He always kept hidden under his uniform something like a good-luck charm that hung by a string over his chest.

He never let it from his person. The day before, Kon happened to get a glimpse of it, and he asked what that thing was that looked like a good-luck charm. Kaneshiro replied that it contained a photograph of his wife and his two daughters. The wife and the two girls, who were still very small, had been caught in the big air raid on the main island in March and were killed. At the time of the raid, his ship was hit by a Grumman from the same enemy task force. The ship went down, and that's when he swam for two days.

Nakamura, beginning to find the story painful, interrupted, "Did you tell him to kill as many Yanks as possible and pay them back for his wife and daughters?"

"Yes, I told him," Kon nodded, and then, in hesitant tones, added, "Do you know what he said? He said the Yanks he might kill probably also had wives and little daughters."

"Then, what did you tell him, Corporal Kon?" Nakamura asked.

"It can't be helped. It's the same for both sides. Kill them. Kill them or they'll kill you. That's what war is like. That's what I told him."

"He won't be the only one to get killed. We'll all get killed." That was Nakamura's reply.

 9

"Now we're going to sing some war songs." With these words, Nakamura jumped up from a hollow under the shore reef where there was a short stretch of grass cover and started walking. The men of his squad, to whom he had

the breaking jewel

given a brief recess in their training for night attacks, were so exhausted they seemed completely drained of vitality. Not only did they lack vitality, but they looked apathetic as they stretched out to rest below the shore reef. Nakamura, recognizing intuitively that in their present shape they wouldn't last until the American landing, said in a low voice to Kon by his side, "I'm going to inject some spirit into them with war songs." He stood up and gave the order.

The light of the moon, once again so brilliant and all-pervading it was frightening, made the white sand on the beach sparkle. Nakamura broke into a trot, as if pursuing his own shadow, and entered the wooded area along the shore. A little clearing had been opened in this area, courtesy of the American bombing. Hidden as they were by a thick growth of trees on all sides, they would probably not be visible here from the sky. The soldiers, energized merely by that one shout from Nakamura, jumped up and ran panting after him to the clearing where they assembled.

They automatically drew up in two ranks and, at a word of command from Nakamura, immediately began to sing. First of all, of course, came "What It Means to Be an Infantryman":

Ten thousand clusters of cherry flowers
Blossom on your collars— *
Storm winds blow the blossoms in Yoshino,
And you, who have been born sons of Yamato,
Will scatter like blossoms in skirmish formation.

*The collar of the infantryman was white, suggesting cherry blossoms. Yoshino was the most celebrated place in Japan for these blossoms. Yamato (in the next line) was a poetic name for Japan.

How many times had Nakamura sung that song since he first joined the army as a regular soldier? And how many more times would he be able to sing it before he died? Of course, he'd go on singing it until he died.

Nakamura, raising his voice with those of his men, looked around them, earnestly singing in the loudest voices they could manage. The clear moonlight illuminated every detail of their faces. To the extreme right of the first rank was bearded Superior Private Active Service Taguchi. Next to him was Sakamoto, also a superior private active service, with a prominent mole on the side of his nose, and one man farther on was Private First Class Yokoyama, who, though a reservist with a wife and children, was the eager beaver to whom Nakamura showed the most kindness and who in turn was the most devoted to him of his men. Behind Yokoyama was Kuronuma, also a reservist private first class, a bachelor, somewhat lazy but of good character. At this point Nakamura stopped his inspection of his men's faces, feeling tears coming to his eyes by the time he reached Kuronuma. Nakamura turned his face away so that the soldiers, facing him as they sang, would not be able to see the tears.

Next after "What It Means to Be an Infantryman" came the war song of the Kwantung army, the one that begins

See, far beyond the early morning clouds,
The endless rise and fall of mountains and rivers.

This war song was always sung second—the order was established. To sing this particular war song on an island in the distant South Pacific may have been inappropriate, but if the Kwantung army was the guardian of the northern regions, this place was a bulwark of the Pacific. Nakamura again led the singing with his loud voice. The men took up the tune at once. By now Nakamura's tears had dried. He was no longer inspecting his men's faces. All he was doing now was singing. After the war song of the Kwantung army came

Surrogates of Heaven, they smite the unjust
Our soldiers, loyal and brave beyond compare.

The song after that was

Here we are in faraway Manchuria,
A thousand miles from home.

Of course, they were not in distant Manchuria. But their homeland was just as many hundreds and even thousands of miles away. This song was depressing, and singing it lowered the spirits. Nakamura sang louder than ever to dispel the gloomy feelings. The men also sang in loud voices. The last song was

Even if the enemy comes in the millions,
They're all a pack of fools,
And even if they're not a pack of fools,
We've got justice on our side.

This war song boosted morale. While Nakamura was singing, he could feel energy welling up inside him. Nakamura reflected on the words of the song even as he sang, though normally he did not think about their meaning. He was thinking: "The Americans are definitely not a pack of fools.

But all the same, we've got justice on our side." The words of the song had never sunk so deeply into his heart.

Suddenly his ears detected that something was wrong. An extraneous noise of some sort was mixed in with the chorus of the men's singing. By the time Nakamura became aware of it, the song was ending. He shouted, "War songs over," aware that the command had come a moment late.

After Nakamura had ordered the men to turn in, he called Private First Class Yamaguchi outside to the shadows under the cliff. Yamaguchi followed him, an anxious look on his face.

"I suppose you know why I sent for you."

Yamaguchi remained silent. He looked at Nakamura, a puzzled expression on his face. Nakamura thought in annoyance, "What's he so sulky about?"

"During that last war song, you were crooning something else, weren't you?" Nakamura kept his voice low, but there was anger in the tone.

"Yamaguchi wasn't crooning, sir. He was humming."

Yamaguchi's self-assured way of speaking irritated Nakamura all the more, but before he could say another word, Yamaguchi continued. "Yamaguchi didn't remember the words very well, so he was humming."

Yamaguchi's excessively calm and composed manner left Nakamura at a loss for words. He looked at Yamaguchi's little face. The strange thought momentarily crossed Nakamura's mind that if Kon's face was appropriately big for a head twice normal size, Yamaguchi's face was the right dimensions for a head half normal size. He resumed his questioning. "But your humming, or whatever you call it, was to a different tune."

the breaking jewel

Yamaguchi denied it. "Sir, that's not true," he said, but an expression of deep concentration passed over his face. Nakamura had no reason to suppose that Yamaguchi was lying. He was much too intelligent—not the sort of person Nakamura liked, but not a man to tell lies. There was nothing Nakamura hated so much as a liar, and if ever he caught one of his men lying, he would always soundly chew him off, then give him a good slapping.

Yamaguchi remained immersed in thought. He even tried humming in a low voice as if to repeat what he had done while the others were singing the war song.

"Mr. Squad Leader, I've figured it out," Yamaguchi said after a while, raising his head and looked squarely at Nakamura. "Without realizing it, Yamaguchi seems to have been humming a different song. It was most unfortunate. He himself is unable to understand how it happened, but it seems to have been a different song . . ."

"What kind of song?"

"A German song, sir." Having made this unexpected reply, Yamaguchi added, as if this was of importance, "It's popular among German soldiers. That's what I was told."

There was always something stilted about Yamaguchi's use of military language, even though he was a regular army soldier, perhaps because his life as a civilian before he joined the army had been rather unusual. Nakamura had heard that from the time he was a boy, Yamaguchi had been a merchant seaman, a deckhand on freighters that sailed to foreign ports.

"How about singing it?"

"I can't sing, sir. Yamaguchi doesn't know the words. It's a German song, and Yamaguchi can't understand it. All he can do is to hum it."

"Go ahead, hum it."

Yamaguchi seemed to hesitate for a moment, only to declare formally in polite language, "Private First Class Yamaguchi, in obedience to the order of His Excellency the Squad Leader, will now hum." He began to hum in a low voice. Without question, this was the same "extraneous noise" Nakamura's ears had detected even while he was singing a war song. Maybe it was just his imagination, but there was definitely something about the tune that linked it to the war song in question. Having finished humming, Yamaguchi was trying to gauge Nakamura's reaction, as the movements of his terror-stricken eyes showed.

"What's the song about?"

"Yamaguchi doesn't really understand it, but he believes it's about a woman who stands before the gate of an army barracks."

"A whore?"

"Apparently so, sir."

Nakamura felt all the more annoyed to think Yamaguchi should have tacked some stupid song onto a war song.

"What's the song called?"

"It's called Lily something or other. It may be the woman's name."

"Your spirit must be pretty slack for you to come out with a song like that while the rest of us were singing war songs."

Yamaguchi remained silent. For a moment Nakamura debated whether he should put some spirit into Yamaguchi with a good slapping. In the end, he held back as a sudden, powerful conviction swept over him that if Yamaguchi's spirit was slack, he would be the one to die.

the breaking jewel

"Where did you learn such a song?"

"It was when I was in Germany. I was working aboard an unscheduled freighter. The ship went to Hamburg. . . . That's when it was."

Nakamura interrupted, "Was it a woman who taught it to you?" His hand started to rise automatically. The hand stopped moving because Yamaguchi's next words were so unexpected.

"No, it was a German soldier, sir. . . . We met at a beer hall. . . . His name was Hans. He was two or three years older than me. . . . He said he was in the tank corps, or whatever they call it. We talked in broken English."

Yamaguchi unquestionably expected to be slapped. He strung out the words piecemeal in a voice shaking with fear, but having managed to say this much, and satisfying himself that Nakamura's hand was not lifted, he went on, "While I was singing the war song a while ago, I was wondering where that German soldier was fighting now. My mind was on Hans . . ."

Nakamura again interrupted him. "And you sang that stupid song about a woman?"

His anger showed in his tone, but there was also something desolate about the tone. That is how his words sounded, even to himself.

Through breaks in the shore reef below the cliff where the two men stood facing each other, white waves could be seen, luminous even in the dark outside the coral reef, and the vast expanse of the thundering ocean, stretching as far as the eye could see, shone pale and dark in the moonlight. Somewhere at the very end of this expanse a light flashed, lightning or perhaps a fired shell, and a moment later there was a rumbling; this time, too, one could not tell if it was thunder or the sound of a shell exploding.

Nakamura went on. "Your spirit is slack." In his heart he said in even harsher tones, "If it's slack, you'll die. You'll be killed. It's as simple as that." Aloud he said only, "Try to put more into it, with everything you've got."

"Yes, sir."

Yamaguchi looked directly at Nakamura. Strength seemed to have come into his eyes. "First Class Private Yamaguchi will put more into everything he does." Yamaguchi's way of speaking was stilted as ever, but a new seriousness had filled his voice.

"Have you been to America?" Nakamura asked, his tone changed. An expression of surprise crossed Yamaguchi's face, but he answered composedly, "Yes, sir, I have." His ship had one time entered port at Tampa in Florida. He added, in tones that rather suggested he was justifying his visit to America, that having been a member of the deck crew of a nonregular freighter, he had gone to every part of the world, wherever the ship went.

"Where else in America have you been?"

Nakamura expected that Yamaguchi would answer either New York or San Francisco, the two places whose names he knew, but Yamaguchi replied, "I didn't go anywhere else in America. The ship was anchored in the harbor for two days, but I went ashore into Tampa only once. That was all." Then, as if anticipating the question that had all but come from Nakamura's mouth—"What did you do there?"—he added, once again composedly, "Somebody took me along for a drink." An older deckhand who had previously been to Tampa and spoke better English than himself had taken him into town. Tampa was full of black people. He had passed any number on the streets. His friend told him that in Tampa there were also a great many swarthy people from the Caribbean region. The waiter at the bar where Yamaguchi was taken was a young white man who greatly resembled his friend Hans. This wasn't surprising, considering his father was a German who had emigrated to America. The bartender was born in exactly the same year as Yamaguchi.

As soon as Yamaguchi finished his account of his experiences in Tampa, Nakamura said, "For all you know, he may be with the landing army."

Yamaguchi looked at him with an expression of astonishment, as if he had not previously considered this possibility.

"He's a young American, just like you. He's a soldier now, and he's going to land here. And once he lands, he's going to kill you." Nakamura spoke the words tauntingly, as if Yamaguchi, standing before him, was the American in question.

Yamaguchi's answer was filled with spirit: "I won't get killed, sir . . . because I'll kill him first."

Another booming sound came from across the water. It was hard to tell whether it was lightning or the explosion of a shell. The sound seemed both to join and to tear apart Yamaguchi and Nakamura.

"You can go hit the sack." Nakamura's tone indicated that he had put a period on the dialogue between them. "You've got to be ready for tomorrow." Then, more to himself than to Yamaguchi, he said, "Tomorrow the fighting begins." His words, spoken in strong tones, were filled with certainty.

Suddenly a surprising thought crossed Nakamura's mind. He realized he had never once actually seen an American. He and the thought for a while confronted each other.

 10

Nakamura's prediction was more or less accurate. Most in the garrison had assumed that a full-scale landing was still some time off, but the next morning there were air attacks and fierce naval bombardment from the task force. They could be interpreted only as the prelude to a full-scale landing.

There is no other way to describe the Americans' landing but as a brutal display of force. The tactics they had successfully employed at one island after another in the Pacific had become even bolder, even more coercive, even more overbearing. In any case, they stormed ashore in a frontal attack on the "main entrance." By now they seemed to give absolutely no consideration to the possibility of a surprise attack or to outsmarting the enemy by attacking from the rear. The intense naval and air bombardment that began the day after Nakamura's "prediction" did indeed announce the commencement of a frontal attack, the assault strategy of the Americans. Ten large aircraft carriers, thirteen battleships and cruisers, more than twenty destroyers, and hundreds of carrier-based planes tightly encircled the landing area. Behind them waited fifty or more transports loaded with tens of thousands of the soldiers who would make the landing. The garrison of the island had received word of the composition of the fleet from headquarters on the main island.

In the face of this force, the total number of combatants the garrison of the island could muster numbered fewer than six thousand men, army and navy combined. They had a total of a dozen or so field guns and howitzers, and seventeen light tanks. Airpower was already nonexistent. The few Zero fighters hidden in the jungle boldly took off as soon as the enemy's full-scale attack began, only immediately to become the prey of domineering Grumman fighters. Exhaling flames, they disappeared into the sea. And that was how it happened that after the Zero fighters had made their suicidal sortie, the airfield, which the garrison had been ordered to defend to the death, was rendered useless by enemy air attacks and naval gunfire that opened huge holes in the runway. The locations of the antiaircraft batteries around the airfield, which at first had boldly joined the battle, were quickly discovered and subjected to concentrated air and naval attack. In the end they were all but silenced.

Watching through a narrow gunport in the pillbox the unbroken naval bombardment and air attacks, Nakamura repeatedly had occasion to think that this would be literally a fight to the death. He and his men had by now moved to fortifications on the shoreline. In this fight to the death, America had high-handedly challenged Japan, and Japan, accepting the challenge, was fighting desperately. This was because Japan and the Japanese could not survive in any other way. The whole outfit had moved to positions on the shore reef, and Nakamura's company, led by the young company commander, who was rated as the outstanding field officer of the whole garrison, had taken up positions at various fortified positions connected by tunnels. The company commander had received from headquarters a sheet of mimeographed paper with the following instructions from the area commandant on the main island:

The enemy appears to be planning a death-defying landing. The success or failure of a new phase of the Greater East Asia War literally hangs on the result of this one battle. Be aware that all the hopes of the armed services and the trust of our whole nation are concentrated on our winning a clear victory. These few days will provide an opportunity that will never come again for us born in the Imperial Land to repay with decisive action the Imperial benevolence. Rise, every one of you, with stern countenance. Officers and men, unite as one, and ready for death, fight bravely until, achieving your long-cherished desire, you obliterate the enemy.

The company commander asked several student-soldiers on his staff to copy by hand these mimeographed instructions, and copies were distributed to squad leaders. Instead of assembling his men and reading the instructions to them, Nakamura passed the paper around, asking the men to read it. Pointing at the word "obliterate," with which he himself was not familiar, he explained—following what he had been told by the company commander—"It means to wipe everybody out." He added that they were to kill the enemy as if they were so much litter, no doubt seizing on the similarity between "obliterate" and "litter." But without explaining their meaning, Nakamura kept to himself the words "achieving your long-cherished desire." Nobody said anything. But

the breaking jewel

after reading the paper, their feelings became one. This they understood without saying a word. They would fight. That was all. This feeling became the source of their strength, enabling Nakamura and his men to endure together the din and shocks of unbroken naval shelling and bombing from the air. Already some reef positions along the coastline, which they had supposed to be invulnerable, had suffered direct hits from the bombardment of offshore battleships and been destroyed. Needless to say, the soldiers inside these positions had all been killed.

The men in Nakamura's squad, however, went on living. They went on living and, early one morning a couple of days later, at last had the pleasure of welcoming ashore the invading army. Nakamura was delighted. He could now meet the challenge head-on. He watched from a gunport as the lines of hundreds of landing craft, amphibious trucks, and amphibious tanks of the invading army pressed forward everywhere toward the coast and thought that it was for this that he had over and over again steeled himself. Fight! Fight to the end! There was no other way either to die or to live. Nakamura repeated this to himself. Repeating gave him strength.

Nakamura already had received word that intensive, concentrated firing from other positions had succeeded in repelling the first wave of the landing. This was perhaps the first victory ever won by a defending garrison over the Americans in all the many assaults against islands of the Pacific. It was an auspicious beginning. After informing his men of the good news, Nakamura asserted, "If we can just hang on, we'll win." He added, "But don't get impatient. Our company doesn't begin firing until the enemy is one hundred fifty meters from the beach line. Until then, don't get carried away and do anything rash. Wait in what in fencing they call the normal position." After saying these words quietly, Nakamura urged his men to reflect in their hearts on the Imperial Rescript to Military Men, adding, "It will calm you and give you courage." So saying, he recited to himself words from the rescript: "Loyal service shall be the basic duty of all members of the military. Members of the military shall observe the proprieties. Members of the military shall honor martial valor. Members of the military shall observe fidelity. Members of the military shall make simplicity their guiding principle." His men also seemed to be repeating these words to themselves in their different ways.

"Now!" Nakamura shouted. At the same moment, the high-pitched shout of the company commander echoed through the tunnels connecting the emplacements: "Commence firing! The targets are the six amphibious landing craft five hundred meters ahead carrying American troops. Straddle fire!" The next instant Nakamura, peering through the gunport, got a momentary but clear glimpse of American soldiers about to jump down from dark green amphibious vehicles into the shallows glittering in morning sunlight close to the sandy beach. He was disconcerted by the face of the very first soldier. It was pitch black. Even at a distance of five hundred meters, he could see it plainly. He took a moment to realize that the man was a "blackie."

All at once the emplacements were engulfed in the roar of every kind of gun the squad possessed, painstakingly concealed up to now in each of the positions—infantry guns, quick-firing guns, trench mortars, grenade throwers, heavy and light machine guns, rifles. At almost the same instant, flashes of light and smoke rose up around the amphibious vehicles. The din of explosions continued. And at more or less the same time, perhaps because the company had succeeded in maintaining contact through the use of shepherd dogs, concentrated fire from artillery positions in the central mountain region began to be directed at the amphibious vehicles at the water's edge.

Nakamura himself fired a light machine gun. His first target was the "blackie" in the lead. Next was a "whitie." He intended it that way. It didn't make any difference to him if they were black or white, what came pouring onto the shore from the amphibious trucks were American soldiers—no, American devils. He fired with his whole body. He had turned himself into a light machine gun and was firing.

Suddenly—had the gunfire brought it on?—a fierce squall struck. It blew and rained so hard it completely blotted out the field of vision. For a moment the gunfire stopped, and a strange silence fell over the battlefield. The only sound was the rain. But the squall cleared immediately, and the gunfire resumed. As he started firing again with his light machine gun, Nakamura's eyes, peering through the gun port, saw six amphibious vehicles at the water's edge, all lying clumsily on their sides and spouting flames. Around them the corpses of American soldiers lay in heaps, looking as if they had fallen one on the other. The sight was as sharply defined as in a photograph. The sight gave new strength to Nakamura, who went on firing his light machine gun, aiming at the American soldiers chaotically running in all directions, seemingly overwhelmed by the garrison's firepower. We're winning! The discovery, the recognition, the emotion surged up in the depths of his new strength.

After the intense and protracted naval shelling and aerial bombardment before the landing, the Americans obviously had not expected that the Japanese army would still possess such firepower, such fighting strength. There obviously had been an element of unpreparedness and inadequate cover in their landing strategy. Or, it might be more accurate to say, they had seriously underrated the Japanese army. The battle that morning was clearly fought on the terms of the superior Japanese forces. With difficulty, the Americans had managed to create a foothold on the beach underneath the cliffs, but their advance had stopped at this point. They evidently were waiting for reinforcements. Nakamura and the others in the unit charged with destroying the enemy at the water's edge had, by combining concentrated rifle and artillery fire, won a major victory. Without question, they had already destroyed a number of the huge heavy tanks the Americans had brought ashore—not to mention amphibious vehicles and amphibious tanks.

 11

    All the same, the American forces bit by bit recovered their firepower and fighting ability. By afternoon they had begun to wrest away control of some of the reef emplacements. First they attacked with tanks. Then, using the tanks as a protective wall, the American infantrymen who had closed in on the emplacements directed automatic rifle fire and hand grenades into the pillboxes through the gun ports. When the Japanese soldiers inside came out to do hand-to-hand fighting, they were mowed down by fire from the tanks. Sometimes the Grumman fighters joined in, strafing from the sky and dropping napalm incendiary bombs that turned the whole area into a sea of flames. These tactics gradually began to show results, and by afternoon the American forces had somehow managed to turn the situation around. In the end they had penetrated as far as the southeast corner of the airfield runway.

A little after three that afternoon, a runner from force headquarters jumped into Nakamura's pillbox with the message "The main strength of our company has received orders to take back the airfield at once. It will attack with full strength." With this brief statement, the company commander had directed the squad leaders and their men to join him. A bare ten minutes later the company, leaving behind necessary personnel who would defend their positions to the death, started to move out. Nakamura turned over his light machine gun to one of his men. He himself carried his favorite Mark 99 rifle, a bayonet flashing at the tip. He also carried a musette bag, a meal of portable rations, and a canteen. Apart from his rifle, his weapons consisted of three hand grenades.

The attack commenced at 16:30. As previously arranged, artillery support from the rear started precisely at that time. The attack was directed at the American troops, headed by tanks, who were already consolidating their positions with sandbags. The grenade thrower squad, led by Nakamura's friend Sergeant Kanō, was ordered to lead the van of the company. The attack at extremely close range with these old-fashioned weapons, in use ever since the Manchurian Incident fifteen years earlier, was fairly effective.

Probably the Americans didn't expect that the Japanese soldiers would still be using such outmoded weapons. After some controlling fire from the Japanese tanks, an attack followed by infantrymen who appeared from behind the tanks, and they suddenly used these small weapons to throw grenades into the sandbagged American positions. Nakamura got a vivid glimpse of panic-stricken American soldiers standing up and attempting to escape in all directions. "Charge!" the company commander ordered. Nakamura also shouted, "Charge!" The Japanese troops began running toward the sandbagged positions ahead. Of course, by this time the Americans were again ready for action, and from each of the sandbagged positions automatic rifles, machine guns, and also weapons that the Japanese could not identify showered frantic, simultaneous bursts of fire at Nakamura and his men as they tried to leap into the American positions. A number of the men fell, but Nakamura, not faltering, ran on. An American soldier crouching in one corner of a position was startled to see a Japanese soldier appear on the other side of sandbags that had been split open by Japanese artillery and rifle fire and were pouring out sand, a detail that Nakamura vividly recalled. When the alarmed American drew himself up to his full height, this was the moment for which Nakamura had repeatedly practiced bayonet charges, and he drove the bayonet, exactly as his training prescribed, into the chest of the American's camouflaged uniform. The American soldier for a moment stood even more upright, only to let out the next instant a death cry, exactly like the screech of the weird birds of the jungle, and fall over backward. As he fell, blood spurted from the chest of his camouflaged uniform, and his face with its goggling eyes could be seen clearly under his helmet. Nakamura had heard that before going into combat, American soldiers used paint to camouflage their faces so as to make it harder to see them. The American's face had evidently been daubed all over with paint that made it look unsightly, even repulsive, in the agony of death.

However, this was as far as the victory went, for either Nakamura or the attacking Japanese army. Nakamura had no time to enjoy either his expertise with the bayonet or the splendid results of his long years of training. Soon afterward a fierce, concentrated American attack began, at first with automatic rifles and then with machine guns, heavy machine guns, antitank guns, and weapons of even larger caliber directed at the Japanese troops who had succeeded in wresting away sandbagged positions. The Americans, doing what they did best, in a matter of seconds threw in tens of thousands of rounds of ammunition, indiscriminately mowing down in a blazing display of firepower people, buildings, trees, and everything else existing on the earth. The Japanese soldiers around Nakamura who had prematurely raised shouts of banzai after managing to occupy a few American sandbagged positions fell haplessly before this power. The sandbagged positions themselves were so thoroughly battered in a matter of moments as to lose all semblance of shape. All the tanks, prize possessions of the Japanese army, had been destroyed; stranded, they had gone up in flames. Nakamura hid in a little hollow between two piles of corpses of Japanese soldiers that had been created in seconds. He committed to memory how the course of the battle had, in an instant, totally changed.

The artillery and rifle firing of the American forces were exactly like angry waves of flame. The angry waves, as if enraged by the unexpectedly determined fighting of the Japanese since morning, swept over the Japanese soldiers, indifferent as to whether they had already turned into corpses or were hiding in gaps between piles of corpses for the brief moments left in their lives. In the meanwhile, the Grumman fighters began relentless, merciless machine-gun strafing, methodically shooting up even the rows of corpses. In an even more terrifying display of power, naval bombardment from warships offshore joined the angry waves of flame. Unable to lift his head even a bare inch from the hollow where he lay, Nakamura had no way of telling where his men might be or what might have happened to them. Were they dead or were they, like Nakamura himself, barely contriving to stay alive? Shrieks and groans spread and filled the depths of the angry waves. The smell of blood, iron, and gunpowder filled the place.

This could no longer be described as a war or as a battle. It was mass slaughter—slaughter in broad daylight. The unfamiliar word "obliterate," which had been contained in the mimeographed page of the area commander's instructions, the word that he had been unable to pronounce, surfaced vaguely before Nakamura's eyes as he lay sunk at the bottom of the angry waves of flame. "I'm really going to meet my end here, like so much litter. I'm going to be burned up like garbage and blotted from the world." Nakamura suddenly realized that this was the meaning of *gyokusai*. Now that the shell that had encased the word had been ripped away by the force of the angry waves of flame, it appeared nakedly before him. It appeared and slammed against his whole body.

He felt as if somebody was calling his name—"Squad Leader Nakamura." He heard it faintly amid the groaning around him. By reflex he stretched out his hand in the direction of the faint voice. His hand touched something lukewarm, yielding, wet, and soft. Without thinking, he started to pull it, only to stop the movement of his hand in horror. Perhaps terror rather than horror would more accurately convey what he felt at that moment. Turning over on his side, he was at last able to see what lay beside him. His eyes registered that his hand was grasping a dark red internal organ protruding from a big hole in the chest of the uniform of the corpse—or soon-to-be corpse—beside him. He withdrew his hand in alarm, at which the corpse—or the body that was about to become one—again faintly called, "Squad Leader Nakamura." Nakamura twisted his body further to get a look at the face. It was Saeki, the reservist whom he had severely slapped for having complained about digging holes for the emplacement. The marks of death plainly showed on his face distorted by agony. He seemed to be only half-conscious.

Saeki's wish that the enemy would hurry up and land, his hope that he would be killed by an enemy bullet, preferring this to enforced and painful labor, had been unexpectedly granted. What was he trying to say after "Squad Leader Nakamura"? Those were his last words. Nakamura vaguely remembered the photographs Saeki had shown him of his cute little boy of about five and his wife, whose most conspicuous feature seemed to be a firm character; but even as he turned over these recollections, he had made up his mind he must escape somehow. He realized instinctively that if he remained there alongside Saeki's corpse, under the spell of his last words, "Squad Leader Nakamura," he would without question be obliterated. An intense fear, worse than any he had ever experienced, suddenly transfixed Nakamura's whole body. Still in a prone position, he began to move. Alternately encouraging and rebuking himself, he murmured,

"One inch more, two inches more, and I'll be out of here, I'll escape."

Luckily for him, the line of corpses extended far beyond the sandbagged positions, and there was a narrow hollow in between. Still prone, he moved slowly, infinitely slowly like an inchworm, through the space. Luckily again, the force of the angry waves of flame had somewhat abated, perhaps because it had been judged that they had already achieved the intended result. This also helped Nakamura make his way to the edge of a wood where tall grasses grew, unharmed except for innumerable scratches on his arms and legs. From there, concealing himself in the tall grass, he would be able to return in comparative safety to his base. For a time, Nakamura moved ahead as intended, carefully choosing the paths he took, and safely made his way back to a point just this side of the base. There he stopped in his tracks as if his whole body had been paralyzed. He could hear voices coming from inside the base, but they were obviously speaking what sounded like English. Nakamura had no idea what they were talking about, but although he had never before heard English spoken in real life, one word caught his ears—"Jap."

He then noticed some corpses of Japanese soldiers that had been unceremoniously thrown out of the position. One of Nakamura's men was among them—Superior Private Taguchi, always conspicuous for his beard. Nakamura thought of tossing a hand grenade into the base from the entrance, but although he had managed with desperate efforts to keep with him the Model 99 rifle he had used to distinguish himself with a model bayonet attack on an American soldier, he had lost the grenades somewhere.

 *12*

All the same, Nakamura managed somehow
to reach by evening of that day the retrenchment position in
the cave that was the easiest to reach of the designated ren-
dezvous points in the central mountains. Those who had survived the failed attempt to annihilate the enemy at the water's
edge—or, it might be more accurate to say, the whole of the
surviving defense forces—had reassembled. They had decided that this was the right moment for the Imperial Army, supported by units that had been kept in reserve that day in the
central area, to stage a counterattack. Their best chance was
to throw all surviving personnel into a traditional night attack, consisting mainly of infiltration raids against the American beachhead. The American landing forces had seized the
shore reefs that until this morning had been the defense positions of the Japanese army and were constructing there
strong beach emplacements, but they were as yet by no
means at full fighting strength. If, taking advantage of this
opportunity, the total strength of all surviving units staged a
night attack, a form of warfare in which the Imperial Army—
and, in particular, this division—prided itself, they could
completely wipe out the American landing force by dawn the
next morning. This plan had long since been decided on, but
in the meantime the force had been given the contradictory
order to wipe out the enemy at the water's edge. Orders were
supreme. They had to be carried out, no matter how severe
they might be on the men, who had no choice but to perform
them. That is what it meant to be military men, to be soldiers.
This awareness, akin to pride, actually had the effect of sus-
taining the soldiers when they flinched. This was true not

only of the ranks. Every survivor, including the officers and noncommissioned officers, shared this feeling. That is how Nakamura perceived them.

He himself was exhausted, and the company commander, whose face looked haggard, had survived the all-day, life-and-death battle in a narrow patch of open ground in the dark of the jungle outside the cave. He gathered around him the men of his command, about to leave for another life and death battle, and gave them parting instructions. The company had suffered many men killed or wounded in the day-long battle, and its numbers had been drastically reduced. Two squad leaders had been killed. One of them, Squad Leader Kanō of the grenade-thrower unit, a man Nakamura knew well, had been at the forefront of the afternoon battle to take back the airfield. Among Nakamura's men, Private First Class Saeki had been killed in the fight to recover the airfield, and Superior Private Taguchi, while defending a position quite literally to the death. Two others had also been killed, for a total of four.

"We have fought well, all day long," the company commander began his instructions in a dejected voice. "But the fight has just begun," he added, lifting his voice. Strength had come back to the tone. "Weren't we the ones who left our homeland so we might become bulwarks of the Pacific? We and the night attack we're about to make will determine the fate of our homeland. The families we've left behind at home—our wives and children, brothers and sisters—all expect us to fight hard and to win. This is no time to hesitate. Hesitating will besmirch the glorious tradition of daring and courage that has been the pride of our division ever since the Russo-Japanese War."

the breaking jewel

After saying these words without a pause, the company commander—who had narrowly missed a direct hit from naval gunfire that afternoon in the battle to recapture the airfield—took a deep breath. He lowered his voice as he went on, as if he was about to disclose a important secret—no, it really *was* an important secret. "Our desperate fight today has already reached the ears of His Majesty, the Supreme Commander. A gracious message has apparently been received stating that His Majesty, expressing great satisfaction in the results of our first encounter with the enemy, has urged us to fight ever harder."

When he had finished his instructions, the company commander ordered all his men to face Japan—at any rate, the direction presumed to be that of Japan—and gave the command "Distant worship of the Palace!" The men all bowed their heads deeply, not removing their helmets. Then the company commander, in changed tones, suddenly began to use familiar language. "How about it, guys, feeling more energetic now?" A stir among the men was their reply to the company commander's words. There was a moment of something like gentleness. "Well then, let's shove off," the company commander said briefly. Then, as if to stiffen the feelings of the men once again, he said, "Imminent departure of the company for a night attack. Targets of the attack are the American landing force shore fortifications." He gave the order in brisk tones, as if had recovered his natural incisiveness. The company began to walk.

The night attack was a failure for two reasons, as Nakamura later analyzed it. The first was that the Americans were already thoroughly familiar with the customary tactics of the Japanese army and fully anticipated that as long as they had sufficient strength, the Japanese would stage night attacks, night after night, beginning with the night of the landing. They were fully prepared. The other reason was that the Americans, contrary to the estimates of the Japanese, had, within a very short time on the day of the landing, brought ashore necessary weapons and supplies, including heavy tanks, and had built a strong beachhead at the point of their landing. The beachhead was anything but flimsy. It was already a powerful bastion.

The Japanese plan called for members of the force to split up and make their way one by one through the jungle to the wooded area bordering the shoreline. There they would reassemble at the last assembly point immediately before taking their first steps on the sandy beach, and from there they would infiltrate and attack simultaneously.

The plan went well up to the moment when they leaped simultaneously onto the beach. The next instant the Americans suddenly raised dozens of flares that made the place as bright as noon. Then came the angry waves of flame—the concentrated shelling and firing from the American forces. It was a repetition of the mass slaughter the Japanese had suffered in broad daylight during the battle on the previous afternoon to recover the airfield, a reenactment of the "obliteration." All Nakamura could do was to repeat what he had done at the airfield. He lay flat on his face, concealing himself among the rapidly forming rows of dead bodies. He had received a wound in the left arm from machine-gun shrapnel scattered down in the angry waves of flame. Moans of pain filled the area. As he lay in the hollow among the corpses, Nakamura could faintly but unmistakably hear these moans under the roar of the waves of flame.

the breaking jewel

Remaining flat on the ground, he gave emergency treatment to his wound.

Even amid the mass slaughter, the Japanese soldiers fought bravely. Nakamura, keeping low, crawled among the rows of corpses. He was not attempting to withdraw to the rear; he was moving forward, hoping somehow to get closer to the enemy positions. Nakamura was not the only one moving forward; every member of his squad, of the whole company, was doing the same. As he moved forward, Nakamura was absolutely certain of this. This conviction reflected his trust in every member of the squad and the whole company. They were trying to get even one yard closer to the enemy, to kill even one more of the enemy. The feelings they shared, the spirit they shared, had become one with the movement of their bodies. Nakamura felt this in every part of his own body. By now he had reached a point that if he ran another twenty or thirty yards, he could charge into the enemy positions, holding aloft the rifle with which he had distinguished himself in the battle to recover the airfield. He in fact barked out the command to his men in the area, "Charge! All members of the squad, follow me!" He was certain that each of them, like himself, was deploying forward, albeit continuing to keep low. He was about to stand when at that moment, amid the roar of the angry waves of flame, an even more deafening noise reverberated, coming in his direction. This could only be the rumble of tanks. The next moment a cluster of heavy tanks could be seen emerging from one side of the enemy positions. You can't fight with bayonets against tanks. To make matters worse, the night attack force was not equipped with the small-size antitank explosives, the kind they called "buns." Just as he was thinking,

"Now we really will be 'obliterated,'" he heard the company commander's shout of "Retreat!" Or perhaps he only thought he heard this command. He himself called out to his men who, he was sure, were around him: "Retreat. Squad, follow me!" He fell back, desperately keeping low, along the hollow between the rows of corpses. At the point where the corpses came to an end, he concealed himself behind the coastal reef at the water's edge until he was finally able to reach the edge of the wood.

After a while, some of his men managed to make their way back. Nakamura led them, walking through the wood in silence, his body bent forward. Only when they had reached the safety of the jungle did Nakamura verify who was with him. Private First Class Yokoyama was first to speak: "Mr. Squad Leader, I'm so glad you're safe." Yokoyama stood out as an eager beaver. His doggedness had won the trust of Nakamura, and he responded to Nakamura's trust by always following faithfully behind him, exactly like an orderly.

"I'm glad about you too," Nakamura responded, then asked, "Where were you?" "Right by your side, sir. Just a little bit farther on and I would've stood up and charged with you. It's too bad." Excitement lingered in his voice, and his words shook a little. Another man reported to Nakamura that Private First Class Yamaguchi had been killed by his side. Yamaguchi, hit by a blast of automatic rifle fire, had tumbled head over heels. "That was all there was to it," the man reported. When Nakamura had the squad sing war songs, Private First Class Yamaguchi had hummed a song he said that German soldiers sang. Nakamura vaguely remembered the humming. Everything in his memory was blurred, as if it had happened years ago. That led him by association to think of

the breaking jewel

the fisherman-soldier from Itoman. He had no need to ask what had happened to Kaneshiro. The fisherman–second class private stood beside him, looking dazed. Nakamura asked, "Are you OK?" but Kaneshiro did not respond. He was incapable of speech. His whole body shook convulsively.

Nakamura's associations went from Kaneshiro to Kon, the noncommissioned officer attached to the squad, who was supposedly keeping an eye on the fisherman and giving him special instructions. Nakamura asked if he was safe. Corporal Kon, sticking out his oversized head from behind a particularly tall palm, answered in deliberate tones, "I'm still alive." The paint had peeled at one place on his helmet where there was a dent. The helmet had evidently been grazed by a bullet or shrapnel.

No sooner had Nakamura reached the first assembly point than he was informed that the company commander had been killed. Superior Private Sakamoto, who stood out among the men not because he was an overachiever like Private First Class Yokoyama but because of the mole on the side of his nose, came forward as soon as he saw Nakamura and informed him. "The company commander died a heroic death, shouting to the last, 'Long Live His Majesty the Emperor!'" He added that it had been decided that the previous commanding officer, the man they called Captain Centipede, would be reappointed as his successor. Naturally Sakamoto referred to him not by the nickname "Captain Centipede" but by his proper name, which he politely prefixed with "His Excellency."

"I can't imagine burying myself in a hole and fighting a war of attrition along with that company commander," Kon interposed, adding, "But Squad Leader, we've both of us managed to stay alive this far. It doesn't matter if the company commander changes—the two of us'll stick it out and never say die. We'll hide in holes. We'll go on living and fighting to the bitter end." Despite his cheerful words, Kon's face looked utterly exhausted. Nakamura expected for a moment after Kon had finished speaking that he would add "And we'll win" in his usual detached but resolute manner, but Kon merely let a faint smile play over his exhausted, massive face and said nothing more.

Nakamura nodded. "That's right, Corporal Kon, you and I will stand fast together." He probably also gave a faint smile. He saw before his eyes the face of the dead company commander. It was not his haggard face when he gave his final instructions. It was his face after they had at last managed to reach the assembly point after the battle to recover the airfield, when for just a moment his youth and vitality had revealed themselves in his expression as he said laughing, as if he had forgotten for this moment his exhaustion, "Sergeant Nakamura, well done. I'm told you gave a model exhibition of bayonetry against an American soldier." It suddenly occurred to Nakamura that this comrade-in-arms had died and would not come back.

 13

The war of attrition dragged on endlessly. According to the Japanese army, the war of attrition had developed exactly as anticipated from using the in-depth strategy of drawing the American forces into the jungle and the mountains and using the caves as retrenchment positions to continue the fighting. A report more closely based on the realities of the fighting would have shown that it was a hopeless prolongation of a doomed situation from which there was no escape. The fighting exposed this state of affairs more plainly by the day.

The Americans, who had expected to dispose of the island in two or three days, found it baffling that the Japanese soldiers, who behaved like madmen, should carry on this completely unexpected war of attrition, hiding in the natural strongholds of caves that could not be destroyed by the powerful naval bombardment and air attacks of which the Americans were so proud and emerging day after day and night after night to stage infiltration attacks. The Japanese raids certainly did not result in real victories, but the number of American casualties steadily mounted. The fighting forces were repeatedly changed. Although the marines, who up to now had constituted the bulk of the forces ashore, were proudly convinced that they were the strongest American troops and normally refused to permit other military forces to intercede, army units had been included in the latest reinforcements, evidence that the marines had sustained such heavy casualties that there were no longer enough of them.

Kon had risked his life to reach force headquarters in the central cave of the ridge, and this information about the American forces was what he had heard from his acquaintance, the Hawaii-bred noncommissioned officer who was in charge of gathering intelligence about the enemy. Kon passed on this information, picked up from enemy radio, to Nakamura and his men. It encouraged them far more, because it was something they had heard directly from Kon, than the formal letters of commendation from force headquarters of which Company Commander Centipede would occasionally inform them, a self-satisfied look on his face, in which they were thanked for their gallant fight. It moved them even more than the news that His Majesty, the Supreme Commander, having been informed of their gallant fight, had again vouchsafed special words of praise.

All the same, the situation for the Japanese forces grew worse by the day. Their infiltration raids had without question caused casualties among the American troops, but the Japanese had suffered many more. The number of dead increased moment by moment, and wounded soldiers filled every cave. The caves no longer resembled anything like retrenchment positions. They had been turned into field hospitals. The pitch black interiors of these caves were filled with the screams and groans of the wounded, the stink of blood, wounds, and pus. The putrid smell from the dead bodies abandoned here and there was unbearable.

Ammunition, food, water, and medicine all were now in short supply. Without ammunition, warfare was impossible, and without food and water, the soldiers could not fight. Without medicine, the wounded soldiers could not be treated. Whether they were "obliterated," the victims of mass slaughter, or died of natural causes, they could only wait for death, the inevitable end result of their starvation. Ugly quarrels started up, especially among seriously wounded soldiers who could not leave the caves on their own power. As long as the quarrels were on the level of "Hand over that potato!" they were still harmless. But it did not take long for them to reach "Give me that lizard tail or I'll use this gun to blast a hole through your chest."

Most serious of all was the shortage of water. Water conservation was indispensable on an island that had so little, but the water stored in the caves had rapidly dwindled after the storage tanks were destroyed by bullets fired into the caves. The Americans had already seized the springs, the only natural source of water. Desperate cries and groans—"Give me some water! I want at least a drink of water before I die"—filled every cave.

Along with the heartrending screams and groans of the wounded soldiers, words of abuse and curses started to be heard in the caves among the seriously wounded, at first in whispers but soon in loud and unabashed tones. With their dying breaths they accused superior officers or their buddies in terms of "You're responsible for getting me into this mess." But others might say, "Pal, I want to kill myself. Lend me your hand grenade. Or shoot me with your gun."

Or somebody else might call out amid the groaning, "At least die like a man. Give three banzais for His Majesty the Emperor, and die decently." "Then, take me somewhere I can decently shout three banzais for His Majesty the Emperor before I die."

Morale had deteriorated. Infiltration attacks continued in every sector, most of them directed against American sentry posts and field tents, but they had turned into attacks by raiding parties whose goal was to seize as many cans of food and canteens as they could carry. Even one can of food or one canteen of water could save for a few fleeting moments the lives of dozens of men in a cave. Just to smell the contents of a can or to have a drop of water on their tongue may have given them the courage to stay alive.

Morale had fallen especially since the American forces,

exasperated because it seemed likely to take forever to secure the island using only such conventional weapons as naval gunfire, air, or tank attacks to mop up the Japanese entrenched in the caves, switched to flamethrowers that poured flames into the caves. Or they would roll into the caves gasoline canisters that were first set afire in order to roast alive or suffocate the Japanese inside. At the same time, they would throw into the caves large quantities of dynamite and other explosives to bring down the roofs of the caves. Or they would mobilize construction machinery, of a kind the Japanese soldiers had never previously seen or even heard of, tanks with steel plates in front that could flatten stones and rocks, collapsing a whole cave or sealing off its mouth, in this way burying alive the Japanese soldiers inside. They also used their powerful flamethrowers to burn away completely the jungle around the caves. This new kind of American tactics was without precedent in the history of the wars fought anywhere in the world, whether in the incineration or suffocation or burial alive of whole units of men or, for that matter, in the destruction of the rock spine of the island and the reduction of the jungle to ashes; it was these tactics of incineration, suffocation, and burial alive that had plunged the Japanese soldiers in the caves into unmitigated terror quite different from the fear aroused by the mass killing caused by artillery and rifle fire. When attacked with these tactics, they had no choice but to abandon even the most strongly constructed retrenchments. Japanese soldiers wandering in the jungle looking for new caves easily became prey to artillery and rifle fire.

The Japanese had completely lost control of the sky and the seas, and now, when they could no longer keep enemy planes away with antiaircraft fire, absolutely no reinforcements or supplies reached the island from the outside. The possibility did not even exist. Fairly soon after the American landing, reinforcements had been sent from the main island. Two hundred or so men in the advance contingent left the main island in the middle of the night aboard landing barges and other vessels that made their way south, from one island to the next. Almost the entire advance contingent had succeeded in landing safely early the next morning on the northern tip of the island, but the main force, thirteen hundred men strong, was subjected on the way over the water to concentrated naval bombardment from the Americans and lost five out of every six men; in the end, only a few more than two hundred men were able to reach the island. These reinforcements soon lost their identity in the deadly confrontation between mass slaughter and infiltration attacks that engulfed the entire island. Later, force headquarters organized a message unit, centered on the sturdy fisherman-soldier conscript from Itoman, that made a break for it over the sea to report to the main island the present situation and the whereabouts of the reinforcements who had landed. The message conveyed to headquarters on the main island the opinion that sending additional reinforcements would serve no useful purpose.

Nearly two months had elapsed since the Americans landed. The situation of the Japanese forces could only be described as desperate. All the same, the Japanese forces, holed up in what were merely caves and could not possibly be called retrenchments, continued their infiltration raids. The American forces, for their part, had blown away the rock spine of the island with powerful shelling and bombing, razed the jungle, and mercilessly poured flames from flamethrowers into the caves, but they still couldn't clean out the Japanese forces. In the meantime, a new development came as a shock to the Japanese continuing their deadly struggle on this little island and perhaps equally to the other side as well. The main strength of the American army had successfully landed at a major base situated to the west of this island—Leyte in the Philippines. The attack and seizure of this small island by the American marines had been carried out in order to facilitate the landing of the main force on Leyte. Now a fierce offensive and defensive battle had begun on Leyte between the Japanese and American troops. If facilitating a landing in the Philippines had been for the Americans the purpose of the battle to capture Peleliu, for the Japanese the desperate defense of the island had been intended solely to prevent the advance and landing of American forces in the Philippines. The American landing at Leyte meant that the main theater of the war had leaped over the heads of the Japanese and American forces even while they continued their life-and-death battle on this little island and was now in the Philippines, a place of major importance. For the Americans, moreover, the Philippines were the key to the invasion of the main Japanese islands by way of Okinawa. For the same reason, the Philippines were vital to the Japanese military, a truly major bulwark for the defense of the Japanese homeland. The little island no longer had the significance of a bulwark of any kind. The great waves of the war had passed over a completely shattered bulwark.

All the same, the deadly combat between the Japanese and American forces continued. The Japanese and Americans

the breaking jewel

were continuing a fight to the death—between mass killings based on a strategy of shelling, flamethrowing, scorched earth, and burial alive and, on the other side, infiltration raids from men dependent on the safety of caves.

 *14*

Communications between garrison head-quarters in the center of the island and the survivors of the failed water's edge attack (like Nakamura and his men) who had been ordered to defend to the death the southern part of the central mountains had long been broken, ever since the Americans burned and captured the jungle separating the two. The most recent information had come when Kon, who probably hoped to get the latest news from his acquaintance the noncommissioned officer from Hawaii, had volunteered to make the journey. Three days later he had brought back valuable information about American casualties, obtained from enemy radio, that had greatly encouraged Nakamura and the others. Afterward, Kon had remained for two days in the cave, on one occasion taking part in an infiltration raid directed by Nakamura. He had succeeded in stabbing to death an American soldier. He said later on, "I'm sure it was a 'blackie' soldier. I couldn't see his face very well because it was black and it was pitch black that night." He added, "The area is swarming with 'blackies.' I'll bet that's because they're using 'blackies' to shield themselves from the bullets."

Kon now set off once again, this time braving a torrential rain, headed for the central ridge where the cave with the force headquarters was located. He had not yet returned. (He wasn't actually "braving a torrential rain" so much as taking advantage of it. Torrential rain and thick fog were now the natural allies that, along with the caves, sheltered the Japanese. In other words, nature—whether the caves or the weather—was now the only weapon protecting the Japanese that they could still employ.)

Kon probably felt that he wanted more information. He decided to accompany Private Second Class Kaneshiro, who, thanks to his powerful physique, had enjoyed the honor of being chosen as a member of a messenger unit that would make the dangerous crossing to the main island. Kon said, "I don't suppose you know the lay of the land, do you? It'd be too bad if you got caught by the Americans. I'll go with you." He talked Company Commander Centipede, still alive at that time, into issuing an order to this effect. Kaneshiro hung on his chest like a amulet the photograph of his wife and daughters, who had been killed in the air attack on the main island in March. The fisherman–private second class, at last at ease in the role of the soldier, managed to make without a mistake the announcement: "Private Second Class Kaneshiro, having received the order to participate in a suicide messenger unit, is now about to leave for force headquarters."

They set out from the cave, all but jumping into the rain, which, luckily for them, had turned fierce. Now that the liaison with force headquarters had been entirely cut by the presence of the Americans in between, Nakamura in the south would have no way of knowing, unless Kon managed somehow to return, if the two men had succeeded in making it to headquarters and if Private Second Class Kaneshiro had been able to go from there safely all the way to the main island.

For all he knew, Kon might have breathed his last a long time ago on the way to headquarters.

Late one night Company Commander Centipede had sent two runners to headquarters. One of them had been killed, and the other had crawled back, seriously wounded. According to his report, delivered painfully with his last breaths, the Americans, after razing the jungle in the middle of the island, had built a road that looked like concrete. It was fully illuminated, and tanks passed back and forth over the road, which was as bright as in broad daylight. There was no possibility of crossing it. All the same, the two of them had attempted to break through, only to be subjected immediately to concentrated fire. His pal had been killed instantly. "I turned back and somehow managed to make it here," he said, and having said this, the survivor also died. After he died, they found in the pockets of his uniform American cigarettes and chocolates, no doubt picked up somewhere in the in-between area. This "extra allowance from Roosevelt" for a time cheered his former pals in the cave. One of them, bringing Nakamura a splinter of chocolate, asked, "How about some?" but Nakamura refused.

The command from force headquarters—"You are to defend to the death the southern part of the middle range of mountains using the retrenchments as your base"—had now lost all meaning. In the first place, the retrenchments that the garrison, including Nakamura's squad, had barely managed to construct in a series of caves with painful digging and toil as future strong points before the Americans landed had been directly assaulted with flamethrowers, phosphorous bombs, napalm bombs, and incendiaries. Either gasoline was poured directly into the caves and then set afire, or else canisters of gasoline that had first been set afire were rolled into the caves. The Japanese soldiers had been driven from the caves by these and every other conceivable variety of barbarous tactics, and then large quantities of dynamite had been thrown in to blow up the caves. After the experience of being driven from fortified caves, the Japanese had discovered in the area innumerable small caves that were suitable for hiding. The few surviving Japanese soldiers of the water's edge annihilation unit—Nakamura and the others who, after the death of the company commander, had taken him as their commander—were continuing the war of attrition from these caves, lying low and, as long as they remained alive, repeating raids of infiltration.

What sustained them now was probably the anger and hatred they directed at the "brutes of American soldiers." Nothing terrified and angered them as much as what were literally the burning-alive attacks of the Americans intended to drive them from the retrenchments. They were beasts, smoked out of their holes by lighting fires. Or if calling them beasts is not an exact simile, they were criminals of the Middle Ages burned alive at the stake. Having experienced mass slaughter under angry waves of flame, it was not the war—even if it caused "obliteration" or worse—that frightened them. Many, especially the seriously wounded who had been left behind, were burned alive in flames that allowed no possibility of rescue. Company Commander Centipede was one of those who died, a pitiful victim cremated at the stake.

The commander's death, by being burned alive, was heroic. He was turned into a human torch when a great quantity of gasoline poured into the cave from the mouth

the breaking jewel

was ignited. He must have realized in a flash that if he were to attempt to escape farther back into the cave while alight, it would increase the danger to the others. So he at once drew out the revolver at his waist and, pressing it against his head, pulled the trigger and killed himself. He fell on the spot. It is possible to interpret this gesture as the act of someone unable to endure the extreme agony of being burned alive or else as merely an act of insanity brought on by an abnormal occurrence, but Nakamura was unwilling to profane the commander's death with such interpretations. If he defiled the commander's death in that way, he himself would be no better than the "American devils" who killed Japanese soldiers inhumanly, not recognizing them as human beings. Never before had he thought the words "American devils" so fitting. Nakamura himself realized this.

Nakamura, who had assumed command over the survivors in place of Company Commander Centipede, addressed his men, now down to a bare forty in number. "I can't forgive the 'American devils' for what they've done. I'm going to have my revenge." He spoke briefly but in solemn tones, as if he were condensing and disgorging a lump that had collected in his chest. This talk took place in the small cave where they had desperately taken refuge the night after they were driven from a retrenchment position by flamethrowing attacks by the Americans. There was no need for him to say very much. What he said was probably what his men, having been tormented by the American soldiers with their flame attacks, felt. They didn't want to die without first taking revenge by killing at least one of them. Probably not only Nakamura but everybody else thought the same. This feeling sustained them.

They spent the whole of the next day making preparations for an attack. This time it would not be just an infiltration raid with bayonets and Japanese swords. The entire body of survivors, thirty-eight men, would stage a night attack with twelve rifles, one light machine gun, five grenade throwers, fifty hand grenades, and four small antitank explosives. Their objective was the American force, including five tanks, that had insolently constructed sandbagged positions immediately below the cave that had formerly been their chief retrenchment position. The cave had later been the scene of immolation by fire and finally was destroyed in a dynamite attack. The American soldiers—no, the American devils—had been responsible for burning alive their comrades and for holding themselves up to mockery.

The night attack was unsuccessful. Several of the Japanese, it is true, had killed an "American devil," but they had been unable to occupy the sandbagged position. With great daring, they had succeeded in laying a small explosive under a tank and had exploded it, but the huge heavy tank did not so much as budge. The Japanese losses, however, were heavy. Of the thirty-eight men, eighteen were killed, and seven, including Nakamura, were wounded.

One of those killed was Private First Class Yokoyama, the eager beaver on whom Nakamura always kept an eye and who, responding to Nakamura's interest, had faithfully performed his role as Nakamura's orderly. Even though Nakamura himself was wounded, he dragged with him Yokoyama, who had received a gunshot wound in the chest and was more dead than alive. At daybreak he found a small cave and the two of them went in, all but collapsing inside.

Nakamura cut open with his bayonet Yokoyama's uniform, soaked with blood, and examined the wound. There was a big hole in his chest, and in the strangely pale light of dawn in the dim cave he could see internal organs faintly moving. "Mr. Squad Leader," First Class Private Yokoyama began under his breath painfully, but nothing followed. A little while later he suddenly said, "Long Live His Majesty the Emperor," and these were his last words. Nakamura realized that this was the first time he had ever heard a soldier, whoever he might be, pronounce these words with his dying breath.

After watching over Private First Class Yokoyama's last moments, Nakamura began to treat his own wound. A hole had been gouged out below his right knee by an automatic rifle bullet. Immediately after being hit, he had tightly rewound his leggings and had applied emergency treatment. Now he took a bandage from his musette bag and treated the wound somewhat more professionally. Then he crawled out of the cave, bruising his hands so badly on the sharp rocks that his palms were covered with blood. He was unable to pull out Yokoyama's body. Even if he had pulled it out, where was he to go with it? After a long while, he made it back to the cave from which they had staged the attack. The first thing he said, as if verifying it to himself, was, "I'm still alive." The faces of the other survivors turned toward him. One of them was Kon's. "I'm still alive, too," he said. He had a growth of beard and his face was emaciated, but that was equally true of Nakamura. He needed no mirror to be sure of it. The two men did not give each other a smile. All they did was nod.

"Did Kaneshiro go to the main island?"

The death of Private First Class Yokoyama, whom he had worried about, prompted Nakamura by association to ask about the fisherman from Itoman to whom Kon had given special training. "He went. He seems to have got there safely" was the brief reply. Then Kon mentioned something quite unexpected: "He said he'd make it back here somehow."

Nakamura, surprised, looked at Kon's face. He deliberately returned the look, then continued, "There's something they call 'the single-minded determination of an idiot.' For all I know, he may already be back." That was his way of speaking.

Nakamura mumbled, "Why should he want to come back?" He added, "It's typical of him." His voice had naturally taken on an angry tone.

"This is what he said. Even if he returned to the main island, his wife and daughters are dead. He has nobody there. And then it's sure to become a battlefield very soon. He couldn't get back to Okinawa, where he came from, but even if he could, sooner or later that would also become a *gyoku-sai* battlefield. That's why he thought it was better to die here with everybody."

"Everybody?" Nakamura asked the question without realizing it.

Kon again looked deliberately at him. "Me. And you, Squad Leader." This was the first time he had used the pronoun *omae** in addressing Nakamura. He continued, changing his tone to one of muttering to himself, "I've also come back."

---

*A pronoun used for either persons of inferior status or else (as here) close friends.

After saying this without emotion, Kon shifted in his seated position. He added, "Over there, they were getting ready to burn the regimental colors."

Nakamura understood at once that by "over there" Kon meant force headquarters. The face of the "warrior," the force commander, slowly surfaced in Nakamura's mind. The face was clearly visible on the screen of his mind, but the screen as a whole had become remote and small, as if viewed from the reverse end of a telescope.

Nakamura started to say something about the force commander, but Kon interrupted, "The present strength is about fifty men in good shape and about seventy seriously wounded, for a grand total of one hundred twenty men. Their only weapons are rifles, and they've got about twenty rounds of ammunition. They plan to stop fighting as a unit and to shift to hit-and-run warfare with the remaining fifty able-bodied men. They intend to hold out as long as possible and to struggle on until they wipe out the American bastards. The seriously wounded who can't fight are expected to kill themselves. . . . That's what it said in the telegram sent to GHQ. Suicides have already been carried out."

Once again Nakamura tried to ask about the force commander. Kon replied in dry tones, "He'll kill himself. Very soon. . . . Maybe he's already killed himself."

Having said this, Kon, in the same dry tones, continued, prefixing his remarks by mentioning that they were what he had heard from his acquaintance, the noncommissioned officer in charge of foreign intelligence. "The main force of the American army has landed in the Philippines, and a fierce battle is being fought there right now. This place is already a forgotten battlefield."

"But I'm going to fight." After some moments of silence Nakamura said these words forcefully, as if throwing his whole body into his refusal to accept Kon's words—the information Kon had transmitted. "How about you, Corporal Kon?"

"I've come back here," Kon said, by way of reply to Nakamura's question.

"What's happened to him?" Nakamura asked, changing his tone. He added, "The noncommissioned officer, the one who told you this story?"

After a moment of silence, Kon replied as if lost in thought, "He's dead. . . . After telling me the news, he went out on a raid and got killed."

 15

Days of artillery fire, burning alive, burial alive, or else direct attack from gunfire, pursuing them from cave to cave, began for Nakamura and Kon. The few remaining soldiers, the remnants of the water's edge fiasco, followed their leaders, two noncommissioned officers. Their movements might best be described as aimless wandering. One after another of the soldiers was killed or wounded or committed suicide after being wounded. What caused the greatest despair, even more than the decrease in or total lack of firearms and ammunition, was the increasingly acute scarcity of food and water. The shortage of water in particular was decisive.

Raids in which even the wounded, including Nakamura himself, took part were still being boldly carried out, but the aim was no longer victory. The raids were staged to capture the canteens from the American soldiers they killed. Of course, the booty was not restricted to canteens. They would steal the blood-smeared packs of American soldiers and snatch from the pockets of their uniforms chocolate bars, crackers, cigarettes, whatever they got their hands on, and then they would run away.

The losses for their side were also very great. Many more of them than of the Americans were killed or wounded. Kon was also wounded, and Nakamura was wounded a second time. Kon's wound in the left arm was slight, but Nakamura had a bullet lodged in his abdomen, and this was unquestionably a serious, life-threatening wound. They say that normally one doesn't recover from a wound to the blind gut. Nakamura had often heard this from years back. A sharp pain from the wound in his abdomen, from which blood literally gushed, lashed his whole body. There was something else that also had taken possession of his whole body—the bottomless fear that with such a wound he could not be saved. Although his consciousness was gradually growing dim, Nakamura strained his voice calling for help. Kon dragged Nakamura's body into a cave that fortunately happened to be near the place where he had been wounded. Nakamura told Kon that he hadn't any more bandages in his musette bag, but there was a thousand-stitch belt. He asked Kon to use the cloth to cover the wound, then to wind it around his abdomen, and to tie it firmly so as to stanch the flow of blood. Kon, although he himself was also wounded, skillfully did what Nakamura had requested. Nakamura had been given the thousand-stitch belt by an old woman who had addressed him at the Shinto shrine on the main island, just before he came to this island. He had completely forgotten about the belt, which she said she had made for her son, and it had remained untouched at the bottom of his pack. He had found it the other day when he used his supply of bandages for his wound in his leg, and he had thought then he might use it as a bandage if ever he got wounded again.

The bleeding may have stopped a little using the thousand-stitch belt to arrest the bleeding. It seemed to him that the pain was also slightly alleviated. Nakamura for a time lay on his side, silent and with his eyes shut. He was no longer capable of estimating how long this "for a time" may have lasted. When he opened his eyes, he could see Kon sitting there beside him. He looked into Nakamura's face as if to ask, without saying anything, if he was all right. Nakamura quietly said to Kon, "You needn't worry any more about me. I don't suppose I have much longer to live. But I'll go on living as long as I can, and if my wound gets even a little better, I'll go out and fight." He muttered this as if to himself. A little while later he added, "If my wound doesn't get any better, all that means is that I'll die. I've kept one grenade at the bottom of my bag. So . . ." After a short pause, he resumed, "Leave me as I am here. Go back to the cave where we were before. There still are some guns and ammunition. You can fight with them. Fight. Even if you're the last man left, keep fighting." The words "Fight and win" all but came from his mouth. That was what he felt, but the last words did not leave his mouth.

Kon listened to Nakamura's words to the end without saying anything. Even after Nakamura had finished talking, he still kept silent, but he held out a dirty sheet of paper covered with tiny print. Nakamura took what was offered him and read the words, holding up the paper to the faint light coming in through a crack in the wall behind Kon.

To the heroic Japanese soldiers!

We have been deeply impressed by the bravery of the Japanese soldiers. We believe that having fought to this point, you have done your duty to the full. It is useless to continue the struggle. You have already completely carried out your mission as Japanese soldiers. Please waste no time in taking these words of advice to an American sentry. We are waiting for all of you. You bear the responsibility for the Japan of the future. Do not throw away your lives uselessly by continuing further resistance that can do no good. What is the Japanese air force doing? Is it not true that not a single plane has come here? The Japanese navy has been cornered in Taiwan and is faced with total destruction. Stop the warfare, the sooner the better, and return to your parents, your brothers, your wives, and your children at home. They are waiting for all of you to return safely. We guarantee we will save the lives of every one of you and send you back to your country unharmed. . . .

Nakamura raised his head and demanded, as loudly as he could, "Are you telling me to become a prisoner?" The hand holding the paper shook. He pushed it back into Kon's hand.

Kon shook his head under his oversize helmet. "It's because I want you to go on living. . . . You're wounded. You can't be saved if you're left here. The American army has doctors. Hospitals too."

Nakamura interrupted him, once again straining his voice. "You probably want to become a prisoner so you can be saved." Anger overflowed, taking possession of his whole body. The words rushed from his lips. "I'm a Japanese. I'm not . . ." Pushing aside a moment of hesitation, he continued, "a Korean like you. I'm not becoming a prisoner."

A violent shock seemed to have assaulted Kon. Pain distorted his features. "Is that what even you say?" His eyes shone with a strange light. With shaking hands, he tore up the piece of paper.

Kon said that the same thing had happened at force headquarters: "Somebody brought me this piece of paper and said the same thing to me. I thought. 'I can't fight in a place like this. I can't die here.' I thought that *this* was where I wanted to fight and to die. That's what I thought, and I came back here." Kon spoke it broken phrases, one piled on the other. Every single word was filled with rage. His words shook with rage.

"And now even you say the same thing." Kon brought to a close his short, piled-up words. His tone had become calm. "I don't intend to fight by your side any longer. I'll fight alone. I'll go on fighting . . ."

Did he follow the last with "and win"? Or did he say "and die"? Nakamura couldn't hear. No, Kon probably did not say anything else. He stared at Nakamura, but his eyes no longer saw him. They saw something else. That is how it seemed to Nakamura.

Kon suddenly blurted out, "Do you know why I became a special volunteer soldier? Shall I tell you? It was because as a Korean, I didn't wanted to be treated any more with contempt by you Japanese. To go on living, treated with contempt . . ." There was a moment of hesitation when he broke off his words, but he immediately resumed. "And it was because I didn't want to be treated with contempt when I got killed."

Kon picked up the gun he had left beside him and stood up. It was a Mark 38 rifle that had been carried by somebody who got killed in the war, but Kon had used this antiquated gun to kill any number of American soldiers. He slowly climbed up to the mouth of the cave through scattered rocks. He turned at this point and said a few more words. "There's one thing I'd like to tell you before I go. My father was killed by you Japanese at the time of the Great Earthquake of 1923."

After a moment of silence, Nakamura spoke, again straining his voice. "Well then, kill me. I'm a Japanese."

After another moment of silence, Kon answered. "You're wounded. I don't kill wounded soldiers, regardless of whether they're American or Japanese. That's my rule in war . . . my principle as a soldier, as a professional soldier."

Each time Kon used the word "I" or "my" he emphasized it. He also emphasized "Japanese soldiers." Nakamura's ears caught the inflection.

There was a sound of gunfire at the mouth of the cave, suggesting somebody was about to come in. Kon, with the agility of a seasoned soldier, adjusted the hold on his gun and quickly ran up the slope scattered with rocks to the mouth of the cave.

No sooner had he disappeared than a fierce barrage of gunfire echoed. It continued for a while before eventually quieting down. There was no sign of anyone trying to enter the cave. And Kon did not return.

A deep feeling of desolation entered Nakamura's heart. Or rather, it took possession of his entire body. He felt as if he was now alone. It was a feeling of having become alone in the whole world. Up until then he had felt that by fighting, by dying, he was linked all the way to Japan, but now that feeling was no longer in him. Cut off from everything, he was lying alone on top of a rock inside a cave. He thought he would kill himself. He thought it was time for him to die.

He wrote a will. Or rather, he imagined the words of a will: "Dear parents, thank you for having brought me up, even though I am an ignoramus and have never repaid your kindness with filial devotion. But I have fought well. I have fought for the sake of His Majesty the Emperor, for our country, and for you my parents, and I have never fought in a way of which I felt ashamed as a military man of the empire. I have nothing to regret. It is unfortunate that because of the wound I have received, I can no longer fight, but please set your minds at rest. I will take my life in an honorable way. . . ."

He had written up to this point in his mind. Then after a little while, he added at the end, "Long Live His Majesty the Emperor!" This was his signature. Or rather, it was something like evidence. He thought: "With this, I ought to be able to get into the Yasukuni Shrine."

But his next thought was, "If only I could get some water. I'd like a drink before I die." His thirst was unbearable. The pain from his wound had again grown severe. No doubt in this heat, maggots had begun to breed in the wound under the thousand-stitch belt he had used in place of a bandage. Nakamura had heard that when maggots start breeding, the pain markedly increases. If he was to die in this steaming hot cave, where it was getting hotter by the moment and he was drenched in sweat, he would at least like a drink of water before he killed himself. He needn't drink to his heart's content. He would be quite happy to die after drinking only as much water as could be contained in the cap of a canteen.

At this moment he sensed the presence of water. Or rather, the smell. He became aware then of a small crevice in the cave wall behind his back, barely big enough for a person to pass through creeping on his hand and knees. It was from there than the smell of water came.

It took a long time—at any rate, it seemed so to him—before Nakamura managed to enter the crevice and crawl through. On the other side was another cave, this one with a dirt floor. The dirt definitely had a dampness about it. He crawled around, searching for water, but there was no water anywhere. Finally, he pressed his mouth to the dirt and stuck out his tongue. His tongue felt the dampness but nothing more. Nakamura shut his eyes. He was gradually losing consciousness. This was a relief from the thirst and the terrible pain, which had grown even worse.

He heard a voice, a woman's. He opened his eyes in surprise. A woman in a filthy dress was bending over his side and looking down at his face. Her face was dark and dirty, but she was unquestionably a woman. The long black hair hanging down on both sides of her face and her dress with its polka-dot pattern, filthy though it was, were proof. The faded light blue of the polka-dot pattern, spattered all over with mud and with dark spots that seemed to be bloodstains, pierced his eyes. The woman spoke. "There's no water here."

"She speaks Japanese," Nakamura thought in astonishment. He had seen women somewhere on the island a couple of times before the Americans landed and assumed she was a native woman.

"There's no water, but I'll give you this," the woman said, offering him a sliver of papaya. Nakamura silently accepted the papaya and pushed it into his mouth. He devoured it ravenously. Or, it might be better to say, he drank it ravenously. When he had finished drinking the papaya, Nakamura made a gesture that undoubtedly conveyed the meaning of "Isn't there any more?" "There's no more," the woman said with a laugh. A dimple appeared on her right cheek. She was middle-aged.

He had managed to regain his composure somewhat. The woman spoke again, apparently having guessed the question on Nakamura's mind. "I'm a P," she said abruptly, then rattled off a list of places where she had worked. These were places Nakamura had never visited, but their names were familiar because they appeared frequently in battle reports. "I've been working at comfort stations in those places," she added. The places she mentioned were mostly islands ranging from the South to the Central Pacific. Some were famous as *gyokusai* islands. "The Americans chased me away, so I came here," she said with a laugh. Again the dimple appeared on her right cheek.

"Are you a Korean P?" Nakamura inquired. "No, I'm a Japanese. A Japanese P. I was born in Osaka, so that makes me an Osaka P." After saying this rather as a joke, she added, "But there were Korean Ps everywhere. They hadn't come the way I did, as a business. A lot of them were forced." These poor women would embrace poor soldiers about to go off to a fight ending in a *gyokusai*. After the soldiers got killed, the women would offer incense and pray for their repose. "You mean it?" Nakamura asked. "Yes, I mean it," the woman replied.

She said she had come here from the main island following *him*. The last word entered Nakamura's ears in italics. She had made her way to the main island after escaping from one island to the next across the Pacific. Just when she began her business there, the war caught up with her. That was the way she talked. During the short time she was in business on the main island, there had been a customer for whom she had fallen from the heart, a rare experience for her. This was her *him*. He was mobilized locally, taken into the army, and sent here. She reasoned that even if she remained on the main island, she was sure to be killed, so she decided to accompany *him,* fight the Americans, and die. And she came here. "You mean it?" Nakamura asked again. "Yes, I mean it," she replied.

The name Kaneshiro flashed across Nakamura's mind but disappeared. "What difference does it make?" Nakamura thought. He asked, "What happened to *him*?" "He got killed. He was dead by the time I got here. He died like a hero, shouting 'Long Life to His Majesty the Emperor.' . . . That's what they told me." The woman again gave a little laugh, but the dimple did not appear.

"And what do you intend to do from now on?" Nakamura asked after a while.

"To die. I came here to die." As she said these words, the expression on the woman's face hardened for a moment. She added, "Until then I'll fight the Americans. I'll fight and avenge *him.*"

Even before Nakamura had the chance to ask, "How do you propose to fight them?" the woman signaled with her eyes at the Mark 38 rifle beside him. "Do you know how to shoot a gun?" Nakamura asked.

"I do," she replied. "My customers were soldiers, and they taught me a lot. If I teased them, they would try to impress me." The woman laughed, and this time the dimple showed on her right cheek. The woman took the gun and stood up.

"Hand over the gun. I'll show you how I fight. I'm an expert marksman," Nakamura shouted. Or rather, that is what he intended to shout, but his voice was weak and blurred. He looked extremely unsightly. He felt it. The woman shook her head.

"He was the first man I ever really loved. This is my war of love. It's my war." There was a strange light in the woman's eyes. She looked at Nakamura with those eyes. "It's my fight, and I'm going to fight it."

With these words, the woman slipped into the crevice through which Nakamura had earlier crawled and disappeared. Had the gun the woman carried misfired? A metallic clatter echoed through the cave.

The island guide, looking up at the rocky mountain that rose above the jungle, said to the Japanese he had been guiding, "There's an interesting story about that place. I wasn't born at the time, so I don't know the facts, but when there was a *gyokusai* by the Japanese army on the island, a Japanese woman who had been a prostitute on the main island followed her lover here. He was a soldier in the garrison. I don't know whether this was before or after the *gyokusai*, but anyway she came here, against all regulations, and she hid with her lover in a cave just below that mountain. The lover got killed there, but after he died, she took his gun and went out to fight. . . ."

Although he said he was born after the war, the guide was well into middle age. He talked in a mixture of clumsy Japanese and somewhat better English. He told the customer, a white-haired Japanese man, "She seems to have kept up quite a fight. She climbed to the top of that mountain and kept firing her gun. She killed a lot of American soldiers down below, and they say she even shot down a plane that was flying overhead."

At that moment a bird with a long tail circled around the mountain, looking like a white glider. The mountain was not very high, but it rose steeply. The guide, following the bird with his eyes as it glided off, said, "The Americans didn't know that this hero was a woman until she was finally shot and rolled down from the top of the mountain."

The guide turned his gaze from the glider-like bird to his customer, the white-haired Japanese. Still in his mixture of broken Japanese and English, he said one more thing. "I wonder, sir, if you can believe a story like that?" Something in his tone suggested that from the start he had dismissed the story as stupid nonsense. There certainly was an overtone of "Stupid people fight stupid wars and get killed."

"I believe it." The Japanese customer replied slowly in his own language. He added, "I was here at the time."

"I," he started to say, then changed it to "we."

"We were here. Here." After a moment he added, "And we fought."